SHARPSHOOTERS GO WEST

While their wives are on their way to New York, the pair of sharpshooters, McGee and Salmon, seize the opportunity to indulge in some travelling themselves. However, they only get as far as the next town when they are robbed, thrown in jail and threatened with being hanged. Then McGee becomes involved with the daughter of the local whiskey supplier. But bandits capture her and duty demands that McGee must try to rescue her. Sharpshooter though he is, this is one confrontation he seems destined to lose . . .

RON WATKINS

SHARPSHOOTERS GO WEST

Complete and Unabridged

LINFORD
Leicester

First published in Great Britain in 2004 by
Robert Hale Limited
London

First Linford Edition
published 2005
by arrangement with
Robert Hale Limited
London

British Library CIP Data

Watkins, Ron, *1930 –*
    Sharpshooters go west.—Large print ed.—
Linford western library
    1. Western stories
    2. Large type books
    I. Title
    823.9'14 [F]

    ISBN 1–84395–919–4

Published by
F. A. Thorpe (Publishing)
Anstey, Leicestershire

Set by Words & Graphics Ltd.
Anstey, Leicestershire
Printed and bound in Great Britain by
T. J. International Ltd., Padstow, Cornwall

This book is printed on acid-free paper

For my grand-daughter,
Laura Sparks,
who reads my novels.

1

The two men faced each other. Raw anger was stamped on their faces.

'Are you calling me a liar?' snarled Salmon. 'I could ride as soon as I could walk.'

'You couldn't walk until you were nine,' snapped McGee.

'What about you?' gritted Salmon.

'What about me?'

'Your mother told me that you couldn't put a sentence together until you were seven.'

'That's right. I remember it well. It was 'one day I'm going to teach that idiot Salmon a lesson'.'

Salmon's face, which had been a deep shade of red, now became an interesting tone of purple.

'If you think you can teach me a lesson, then go ahead.'

'Are you calling me?' McGee spat the words out.

'You've got it. Unless you want to back down.'

'I can draw my gun quicker than you can blink,' said McGee. 'If you're calling me, you'd better start counting. That is if you can count up to five.'

'Why not make it ten? Although come to think of it your eyes are not too good. Maybe you won't be able to see me at twenty yards.'

'I could see enough of you at a hundred yards to shoot your ears off.'

'If you've got any final words, now is the time to say them.'

'You don't need any final words. What you need is a final prayer.'

'All right. Put your action where your mouth is.'

The two turned so that they were standing back to back. Salmon was a head and shoulders taller than McGee. Both were dressed in the clothes they wore for riding the range, the only visible difference was that McGee was wearing a white hat while Salmon's was black.

'Ready?' snapped Salmon.

'Start counting,' countered McGee.

'One . . . two . . . three . . . '

As he counted the two walked slowly away from each other. Both held their hands poised a few inches above their revolvers.

' . . . six . . . seven . . . eight . . . ' intoned Salmon.

The distance between them had increased to about sixteen yards. Both took deliberate steps as Salmon spat out each number.

'Nine.' This time he raised his voice and shouted it out.

The moment of truth had arrived. There was a split second before Salmon yelled: 'Ten.'

For a big man he swung round with startling rapidity. McGee had also spun round. They reached for the guns simultaneously. It was impossible to say in the blur of their individual movements which had drawn first. The *cracks* of the Colts also seemed to come at the same time. It was also difficult to say, as their hats rose into the air, which one had been the first to knock the other's headgear off.

The couple of dozen or so in the audience burst into rapturous applause. They had never seen such shooting before.

'That was great,' said an old-timer. 'If you two boys will come to my farm and shoot some of the crows I'll give you a dime for each crow you kill.'

McGee, who was collecting dona-tions from the small audience in his hat, ignored the offer.

He came to a small boy who insisted on examining his hat before he put a nickel inside. 'This hole isn't in the middle,' he remarked, critically.

'I'll tell you what I'll do,' said McGee. 'Have you heard of William Tell?'

'No,' confessed the boy.

'He put an apple on his son's head while he shot it off. Now if you'll stand over by that tree with an apple on your head, I'll shoot it off. This time I'll hit it in the middle.'

'You're not going to shoot anything off my head,' cried the boy, panic having set in. He followed his statement by turning on his heel and haring away from the clearing where the sharpshooters had been demonstrating their skills.

Ten minutes later the small crowd had dispersed and McGee had counted the money.

'How much?' enquired Salmon.

'Four dollars and seventy cents,' said McGee with more than a hint of disgust in his voice.

'That's hardly enough to buy us a few drinks down at the saloon,' said Salmon. His air of expectancy had also changed to disgust.

'It's not enough to play a few hands of poker,' retorted McGee.

'I was looking forward to calling in the saloon,' said Salmon.

'Of course if I took all the money and joined in a game of cards I'm sure I could double it in no time,' said McGee, thoughtfully.

'No, you don't,' said Salmon, quickly. 'I'll have my share now.' He suited his action to his words by snatching two dollars and a handful of cents from his companion.

'We can't even borrow any money from our wives,' said McGee as he started to roll a cigarette.

'How long do you think they'll be away for?' demanded Salmon.

'Two months. Three months,' replied McGee irritably.

'Jill didn't say that they would be away as long as that,' said a shocked Salmon.

'She didn't want to worry you,' McGee pointed out, reasonably. 'Look at it this way. They've gone to New York to show our babies to their parents and grandparents. They're not going to rush back. It'll probably be the last chance their families will have to see their children.'

'Jill said they'd only be away for a few

weeks,' said Salmon, stubbornly.

'That's what I said,' stated McGee, placatingly. 'Eight weeks. Ten weeks.'

Salmon regarded him suspiciously. 'What have you got on your mind?'

'Me? Nothing,' said McGee, as innocent as a choirboy. 'What makes you think I've got something on my mind?'

'I haven't known you for these past years without being able to tell when you're up to something.'

'Well I did have one idea,' said McGee. He set a light to his cigarette.

'All right, I might as well hear it.' Salmon, too, began to make a cigarette.

'We could go to Chicago,' McGee stated calmly.

'What!' Salmon was so startled by the suggestion that he almost tipped his tin of tobacco.

'It makes sense,' said his partner, persuasively. 'Our wives will be away for a few months. We'll go to Chicago, where we'll make a fortune with our sharp-shooting. Think of the surprise on their faces when they come back and we give them the money.'

'I'm thinking of the surprise on your face when I say no,' retorted Salmon.

'Is that your last word?' demanded McGee.

'That's my last word,' replied Salmon.

2

Three days later the two set out on the trail for Chicago. McGee had spent much of his time and energy in cajoling, wheedling, and promising — all, it seemed, to no avail. Salmon had stubbornly stuck to his refusal to entertain the thought of travelling to Chicago. While McGee's arguments had varied — in most cases he had portrayed their possible existence in Chicago as an idyllic one where onlookers would crowd to see their shooting skills and they would be able to collect dozens of dollars each time they put on a show — Salmon's had usually countered with a monosyllabic 'No.'

On occasions Salmon had ventured the opinion that: 'Chicago is known as sin city. It's the last place on earth that Jill would want me to go to.'

An exasperated McGee had eventually conceded.

'All right. We won't tell her we've been there.'

'But that would mean lying to Jill,' stated a shocked Salmon.

McGee felt that he was on the point of tearing his hair.

'Give me strength,' he muttered, before turning away and riding off on the range.

In the end the argument that made Salmon change his mind came not from McGee but from one of the cowboys who worked on the same ranch. His name was Weston. He was a married man who was known to be careful with his money. He never joined in the games of cards which the cowboys indulged in on most weekends when they went into town and had a few drinks in a saloon. Nor would he join in the other innocent gambling games where the cowboys would bet whether a persistent fly would land on a window or not. Or who would be the next cowboy to come into the ranch. Nearly all the bets were of small amounts and so nobody would lose much money by joining in. But even these harmless activities were ignored by Weston.

As a result he, too, was largely ignored by the rest of the cowboys. They had long ago given up trying to persuade him to come down to the saloon. They knew he was married and so would not be joining the half a dozen cowboys who were single and who would be invariably trying to sweet-talk the ladies who frequented the saloon. In fact his words of advice to the single cowboys to, 'Make sure you don't catch syphilis', didn't exactly endear him to them.

Salmon and McGee were therefore surprised when Weston approached them. His face radiated *bonhomie*.

'Hullo boys,' he greeted them.

The two companions regarded him suspiciously. The warmth of the greeting seemed out of character. Indeed the fact that he had greeted them at all was definitely unusual. Weston always went about his daily routine of riding the range with the minimum of communication between himself and the other cowboys.

'You two boys are different from the others,' Weston began. The two were puzzled by the opening gambit, but didn't disagree with it. The truth was, they, too regarded themselves as different from other cowboys. They had only been cowboys for about six months. Before they came to Stoneville they had been sharpshooters in a circus in New York. Unfortunately they had joined in a game of cards with a local gambler known as Charlie the Hook. The result had been the two had lost several thousand dollars, which they owed to Charlie the Hook. They were unable to pay the money. Other gamblers who had found themselves in the same position had invariably been discovered floating face downwards in the Hudson River. So the duo took the only course of action open to them. They fled from New York.

'Yes, I suppose we are different,' said McGee, cautiously, wondering what was coming next.

'That's why I want to show you this,' said Weston. He took out a handkerchief. McGee regarded it suspiciously. It was a carefully laundered handkerchief. Not the kind of grubby piece of material which he usually carried around with him and which fulfilled a dual service as something to apply to his nose and also with which to clean his guns. To his surprise Weston opened up the handkerchief and proudly displayed what had been concealed inside. It was a gleaming brooch. 'They are real diamonds,' said Weston, his voice bursting with pride.

'It's very pretty,' concurred McGee, having given it a cursory examination.

'My brother-in-law bought it for me in Chicago. It's my wife's thirtieth birthday on Saturday.'

Surprisingly Salmon was the one who was the more impressed with the brooch.

'It's lovely,' he said, admiringly.

McGee was on the point of walking away when he was struck by an idea.

'How much did it cost?'

Weston hesitated before replying:

'I suppose there's no harm in telling you boys. You won't tell the others though, will you?'

They agreed that they wouldn't tell the others.

'It cost six hundred dollars.'

Salmon was still admiring it.

'That's a lot of money.' He shook his head to indicate that such a sum was beyond his wildest consideration.

'It took me a long time to save it up.' Weston folded the handkerchief carefully and put it in his pouch.

A few moments later McGee followed up the look of desire on Salmon's face when he had examined the brooch with the question:

'You would have liked to buy a brooch like that for Jill, wouldn't you?'

'Of course I would,' snapped Salmon.

'But where would I get six hundred dollars?'

'In Chicago,' announced McGee, triumphantly.

For the first time Salmon was willing to listen to his companion's arguments. McGee was persuasive. He pointed out all the advantages of giving up their present lowly paid occupation and going to the city, where they could share in its prosperity.

'It's a growing city,' concluded McGee. 'We'll make a fortune there.'

'You'd better be right,' said Salmon.

3

'How far is Chicago?' enquired Salmon.

'Quite a way,' replied McGee.

'You know I don't like riding for long distances,' said Salmon. 'I get saddle sores.'

'Don't worry. I've solved the problem,' said McGee.

'How?' demanded Salmon, suspiciously. He had known McGee long enough to be wary of any decisions McGee made which affected him.

'I've arranged a seat for you for some of the way.'

'A seat? We can't go by train, there's no railroad running from here.'

'I'm not talking about a train. I'm talking about the stage.'

'We're going by stage to Chicago?' demanded an incredulous Salmon.

'Well, not all the way. The stage only goes part of the way. But we'll go with it as far as it goes.'

'We'll both have seats on the stage.' Salmon had brightened on hearing the news.

'Exactly. I've booked them.'

'But seats on the stage cost money. And we've only got the twenty dollars each that Johnson gave us when he paid us off.'

'The beauty of the arrangement is that it won't cost us a dollar,' stated McGee.

Suspicion was Salmon's instant reaction.

'What's the catch?' he demanded.

'The stage has been held up recently. They say that it's the Staple gang who're responsible.'

'So?'

'I told the stage driver that we're sharpshooters. He said we'd be welcome on the stage as extra protection for the passengers.'

Salmon mulled over the announcement. He obviously wasn't too happy about it.

'Who are this Staple gang?'

'Oh, just some outlaws,' said McGee, dismissively.

'Just some outlaws.' Salmon raised his voice. 'Do you know that outlaws carry guns. If they use them then people are likely to be shot. If we're inside the stage we could be one of their targets.'

'Well, of course if you don't want to go to Chicago to buy a nice present for Jill ... ' McGee's dismissive gesture indicated that he was prepared to wash his hands of the whole business.

'Well, I don't know. It could be dangerous.' Salmon scratched his head while reconsidering the situation.

'Of course, there's another thing,' prompted McGee.

'What's that?'

'We've already been paid off by Johnson. If we stay in this one-horse town we'll have to find another job.'

Salmon gave the matter further thought.

'I suppose when we're inside the

stage we'll be able to keep a keen look-out for the outlaws.'

'Exactly. The chances are they won't attack anyhow. They've already ambushed the stage once. They know there's very little of value on it. There's only the mail and as you say this is a one-horse town and so there's hardly any valuable mail on the stage.'

Salmon began to relax visibly.

'So the fact that they've held the stage up once could be a good thing for us travellers.'

'You've got it.'

Having recovered from his initial misgivings Salmon managed a smile.

'Then Chicago, here we come.'

'We've got to be at the staging post by nine o'clock,' McGee informed him.

The following morning when they rode up the main street of Stoneville they could see the stage was standing outside the bank. A heavy metal chest was being carried from the bank and loaded on to it.

'That looks as though there's money

inside it,' stated Salmon, as they drew near.

'So what?' replied McGee.

'So if the stage is carrying money to another bank it means that it is more likely to be held up,' stated a worried Salmon.

'We know there's probably money being taken to another bank,' concurred McGee. 'But that doesn't mean to say that the Staple gang know it.'

The heavy chest had been loaded. The two bank assistants returned to their duties in the bank. The stagedriver appraised the two approaching riders.

'You two are the sharpshooters?' he said, seeking confirmation.

'That's right,' said McGee.

'Tie your horses behind the stage. Then you can get inside,' He addressed the remark to McGee.

'What about me?' demanded Salmon.

'Didn't your friend tell you? You'll be up on the buckboard with me. You'll be riding shotgun.'

4

There were six people inside the stage as it started on its way to the town of Herford, which was twenty miles away. There were three men and three women. Two of the couples were obviously married. One was a young farmer and his wife, who judging by their accents came from somewhere in Scandinavia. The other couple, who were slightly older, were American and after the introductions the husband stated that he, too, was a farmer. The fifth person was a well-dressed grey-haired middle-aged man who to McGee's critical eye could be a bank manager or some other business man. McGee had lived in New York for several years before travelling to Stoneville and he reckoned he could spot a rich businessman a mile away. McGee speculated that perhaps the traveller, who introduced himself as Horace Pope, was travelling with the heavy chest which had been loaded from the bank. Yes, that seemed a likely explanation. Maybe Mr Pope would be working in the new bank, wherever that would be.

The conversation inside the stage was largely dominated by the two farmers. Their topic of conversation — the rising prices of corn, pigs, cattle and various other livestock on a farm held no interest for McGee. The conversation between the two women — the prices of ladies' garments also left him cold. Mr Pope obviously didn't intend taking part in the conversation since, shortly after the stage had started, he had produced a leather book bound in red which, judging from its thickness, would keep him busily reading until the end of the journey. Since McGee was seated opposite him he had no chance of sneaking a glance at the book's title. Instead he chose one of the other options open to him — he closed his eyes and went to sleep.

When McGee awoke he was aware that the horses were pulling up. Surely they couldn't have arrived at Herford already. When he glanced out through the window the cause of their stoppage was apparent — they had arrived at the half-way staging post. Here, the horses could be watered while the travellers on the stage could have a cup of coffee and a bowl of soup if they needed it.

Salmon was already standing by the horses when McGee descended from the stage.

'Let's have a cup of coffee,' suggested McGee.

'I'm not speaking to you,' said a surly Salmon.

McGee refrained from pointing out that Salmon had already spoken to him. Instead he said:

'There's no need to be sore because you're riding on the buckboard. It's the best seat on the journey. I've got two farmers and their wives inside and all they're talking about is the price of livestock and clothes.'

Salmon brightened when he realized that McGee, in choosing to ride inside the stage, wasn't having the best of the deal.

'All right, I'll have a cup of coffee,' he concurred.

Inside the building the farmers and their wives were already seated together at a long table with bowls of soup in front of them. There was no sign of the businessman. McGee approached a small counter behind which stood a buxom woman in a white apron. He ordered the coffees.

'The soup smells nice,' said Salmon.

'It's onion and rabbit soup,' she explained.

'We'll have one each,' said Salmon.

McGee, relieved that his friend was no longer taking umbrage about travelling on the buckboard, nodded in agreement.

The proprietor, who was as thin as his wife was plump, brought the soups over to them.

'I've suppose you've heard about the holdup . . . ' he began.

'Yes, we've heard something about it,' said McGee. He began to break up the thick homemade bread and dip it into his soup.

'Where exactly was it?' demanded Salmon.

'About three miles this side of Herford. There's a narrow valley there which is about a mile long. It's a perfect place for an ambush. I'd keep your eyes open when the stage goes through it,' advised the proprietor, as he turned back towards the kitchen.

'Well at least we know where the hold-up is likely to take place,' said McGee.

'I thought you said there wasn't likely to be a hold-up,' said Salmon, with more than a little hostility in his voice.

'I said the chances were that there probably wouldn't be a hold-up,' said McGee, trying to sound as convincing as a politician on election day.

Salmon, who had suddenly lost his

appetite for the soup, pushed the bowl away.

'If you don't want it, I'll have it,' said McGee.

'I should never have let you talk me into coming on this trip.' Salmon stood up. 'We could have stayed in Stoneville until our wives came back.'

The four others, who were seated at the far end of the long table, glanced up interestedly at the sounds of the quarrel.

'Everything will be all right when we get to Chicago,' promised McGee.

Whatever Salmon was going to reply was never uttered. Three men burst into the room. They all held their guns at the ready. McGee had never seen two of them before. But the third he recognized as Horace Pope. He, too, held a revolver in his hand. He was obviously the spokesman.

'This the end of the line for you travellers,' he stated.

5

Herford was a bustling town. True, the railroad hadn't yet arrived there, but there was talk that it would arrive in a year or two. Like most towns in the West it owed its new-found prosperity to the cattle which roamed the prairie. The dreaded barbed wire fences hadn't yet arrived and the cattle were free to roam the range. No one even contemplated fencing in the land. Animals had been free to roam at will when they were in the form of buffaloes which had been hunted by the Indians. Now they were broad-horned cattle with a distinguishing mark emblazoned on them. They were as familiar in the prairie around Herford as the cowboys who rounded them up. Shortly all this was due to change.

The last thing on the sheriff's mind at present was the cattle on the open range. He was concerned about the stage. Or rather where it was, since it had failed to arrive.

'It's two hours late.' The sheriff, Tom Milton, addressed his remark to his deputy, Frank Gardner.

'I know.' Both men's faces wore the same worried frowns.

'Of course there could be a simple explanation. Maybe one of the horses has lost a shoe.' Tom was ever an optimist. He had survived as a sheriff for over ten years. Even during the worst of the Indian wars he had maintained a demeanour of calmness and hope which had helped the community to survive through those turbulent times.

'There was a robbery on the stage a couple of months ago, this could be another one.' The deputy, who was twenty years younger than his boss, was a realist.

The sheriff sighed. 'I suppose you're right. At least we know the routine by now.'

'You want me to form a posse?'

'That's the general idea.'

'It's not easy, you know that. The usual members of the posse, the cowboys, are all out on the range.'

'See if you can find half a dozen men from those who are out of work. Offer them ten dollars each.'

Frank left the office. He had little hope of raising the half-dozen men the sheriff had demanded. On the previous occasion when the stage had been attacked he had been able to raise a posse from the largest ranch in the vicinity — Glenn Chaucer's. He had ridden out to Chaucer's spread and the boss had instantly supplied him with half a dozen cowboys. The reason why Chaucer had supplied the cowboys with alacrity was because it was the first time he had ever been asked to help to supply a posse. There was also the further reason that he had been friendly with the sheriff, Tom Milton, for many years. In fact they had both arrived at Herford at the same time, when the town was merely a trading post. A great deal of water had gone under the town's bridge since that time, but for the sake of friendship Chaucer had agreed to Frank's request.

Tom had ridden out with the six cowboys. Their aim was to find the stage and bring it in safely to the town. The cowboys had little realization of the danger that could be ahead. At last they came across the stage. The passengers had all been robbed but were unharmed. The robbers had set the horses free so those on the stage had sat there waiting for help to arrive. Tom's relief at finding that nobody had been killed was short-lived. One of the cowboys, whose eyesight was keener than the others, spotted the robbers riding away in the far distance. He informed the others. Before Tom could stop them the cowboys had ridden after the robbers. Tom had been forced to follow. They had caught up with the robbers — there were six of the them — and a gunfight had ensued. One of the robbers had been killed. But three of Chaucer's cowboys had also lost their lives. Which was the reason why Tom knew he couldn't approach Chaucer for any of his cowboys again.

Regretfully he came to the only obvious conclusion. He'd call at the saloons in order to try to form a posse. But he knew that his chances were slim.

6

A couple of hours previously Salmon and McGee had arrived at the conclusion that their chances of survival were slim. They had faced gunmen before and they recognized the faces of killers when they saw them. Now that Horace Pope held a gun in his hand McGee realized that even he was a seasoned killer. It didn't take a genius to work out that the only thing that stood in the way of the outlaws taking the chest, which was now sitting on the floor of the room, and making a successful disappearance into some town or other was the fact that the husband and wife who ran the stage and the five passengers would be able to identify them to the law. The obvious answer would be to kill all the witnesses. Which course of action unfortunately included Salmon and McGee.

The *click* of Pope's revolver told the assembled company that they were staring death in the face. Salmon closed his eyes. He was determined that when he died he would have a mental picture of his wife, Jill, to take with him to whatever part of eternity he might be heading. Salmon succeeded in conjuring up the picture of his beloved. He held it reverently in his imagination while he waited for the inevitable explosion.

To his surprise the sound he heard was not the roar of a revolver, but McGee's voice.

'We're outlaws like yourselves,' said McGee.

What was McGee saying? Salmon struggled to make sense of his friend's remark.

'So there's no point in killing us,' pursued McGee.

Salmon opened his eyes. He was in time to see the man who looked like a banker, smile. Indeed the smile grew wider and wider. Even the other two outlaws, who looked as though their habitual expressions were the scowls which they now presented to the world, eased their faces into the semblance of grins.

'So you two are outlaws,' said Pope. 'What are your names?'

'McGee and Salmon,' came the answer.

'Well, McGee and Salmon, I was working for the Pinkerton Detective Agency in Chicago before I found that this way of life was far more profitable. While I was working for the agency I got to know most of the wanted outlaws. And I'm pretty sure that none of them was called McGee or Salmon.'

Salmon's hopes, which had started to rise when McGee had made his statement, now plummeted back down to his boots.

'The agency probably wouldn't have known about us,' stated McGee. 'We operated in New York. That's where we are wanted.'

Salmon reflected that the last state-ment was quite true. Charlie the Hook wanted them to pay a small matter of $5,000 which they owed him for gambling debts.

'Yes, it's possible that if you were operating in New York, the agency wouldn't have heard about you two.' Pope scratched his chin thoughtfully.

'Let's shoot them all and get away from here,' said one of the outlaws, whose patience was running thin.

'You could do with a couple of extra guns,' said McGee. 'Three of you aren't going to last very long — not if you intend pulling any more robberies.'

'We can shoot,' said Salmon, who felt that it was about time he made some contribution to McGee's attempt to get them to survive.

Pope again permitted himself one of his smiles.

'I'm afraid I can't give you two guns with bullets in them in order for you to prove it. You see, you might turn them on us.'

'At least we can show you how fast we can draw,' said McGee. 'That would

35

be half the proof you would need.'

'Ye-es, I suppose we could do that.' Pope nodded his approval at the suggestion. He turned to one of the outlaws, 'Cranmer, give them their guns back.'

The outlaw who was so addressed picked up McGee's and Salmon's guns which had been tossed on the floor when they had been disarmed. He emptied the bullets out. Then he handed the guns back to the duo.

McGee and Salmon slipped the guns back into their holsters. McGee nodded to Salmon. They turned until they were back to back. Slowly they began to walk away from each other.

The room was a long room and as they walked McGee counted.

'One, two three . . .'

The onlookers watched with interest. Even the two outlaws who had been in a hurry to leave the vicinity of the staging post followed the progress of the two keenly.

'Seven, eight, nine . . .'

36

McGee was still counting. As he counted he was coming nearer to the door leading outside to the yard. The door was ajar.

'Ten, eleven . . . '

McGee was now only a few yards from the door. Instead of going for his gun as everyone was expecting, McGee dived through the door.

His sudden movement took everybody by surprise. Although the three outlaws were holding their guns in their hands, the weapons had been held loosely. It therefore took them a couple of seconds to restore them to firing position. During that time McGee had disappeared.

'After him!' screamed Pope.

McGee had a slight start. He took advantage of it and dived round the corner of the building. The stagecoach was standing expectantly, waiting for the driver to start on its way. More importantly, McGee's horse was also waiting expectantly to start on its way towards Herford.

McGee's expertise in riding which he had gained while working for Marney's Wild West Show had never helped him more. He vaulted expertly on to the horse's back. When the gunmen came out through the door McGee was already half-way towards the low wall which surrounded the stage post. The gunmen tried a couple of speculative shots at the rapidly disappearing form. McGee's horse, spurred on by the gunfire, flew over the wall. McGee knew when they landed the other side of the wall that he had won round one. This was only the beginning. His friend, Salmon, was still inside. The question was, how was he going to get him out?

7

When the two gunmen returned to the room their faces told Pope about their lack of success in preventing McGee from escaping.

'He was too quick,' explained the outlaw named Cranmer. 'He jumped on the horse and he was off in a flash. I've never seen such slick riding.'

'We used to work in a circus,' explained Salmon, with barely concealed pride in his voice. 'We were expert horsemen.'

'As well as expert sharpshooters, I suppose,' snarled Pope, who was purple with rage.

'That's right,' confirmed Salmon.

Pope struggled with his anger. Eventually his colour returned to normal and he breathed evenly.

'All right.' He addressed the two outlaws. 'We have to assume that

McGee is on his way to Herford. It will take him some time to get there. So we've plenty of time. The first thing to do is to open this thing.' He addressed the next remark to the stage-driver. 'Where's the key?'

The driver handed it over.

Pope opened the chest. All those in the room stared, fascinated, at the money in the chest.

'Yes, look at it,' said Pope, triumphantly. 'Twenty thousand dollars. You'll never see such money again in your lives. Not that you're all going to live long enough anyhow to see any more money.'

Salmon, whose hopes had been raised by McGee's escape found himself again plunged in the depths of black despair. So the outlaw still intended shooting them all. If only he could get to grips with the outlaw he would strangle him with his bare hands. It wasn't wishful thinking since one of his acts in the circus had involved bending iron bars and another had been to rip a pack of cards into four.

'Stay where you are.' Pope snapped out the command.

Salmon wasn't even aware that he had involuntarily taken a pace forward in response to his unconscious desire for revenge. He stopped in his tracks.

'That's better,' said Pope. He waved the gun around the assembled company. 'Nobody moves until I give the orders, do you understand?'

There was a mumbled chorus in which the word 'yes' could be faintly distinguished.

'Right,' said Pope. He pointed his revolver at the man who ran the staging post. 'Fetch me three saddle-bags. If you're not back in five minutes, I'll shoot your wife. Assuming she is your wife,' he added with a chuckle.

'Of course I'm his wife,' snapped the woman standing beside him. 'I've been married to Glyn for eight years.'

Pope indicated to Glyn by gesturing with his gun that he should get on with the task. To emphasize the point Pope took out his watch and glanced at it meaningfully. Glyn scuttled out through the door.

The atmosphere in the room had changed subtly. The fact that Pope had chuckled at his joke had seemed to affect the other two outlaws. There had been a noticeable change in their attitudes. It was obvious to Salmon that Pope ruled them completely. In fact both of them appeared to be dead scared of Pope. Once, however, he had cracked his joke their demeanour changed. One of them even ventured a comment.

'Do you think all the money is in there?' ventured the smaller of the two outlaws. He had a distinguishing scar down the right side of his face. Salmon guessed it had come as a result of a knife fight with somebody or other in which the outlaw had seemed to have come off second best.

'Well, I'm not going to count it.' Pope's air of *bonhomie* seemed to be continuing. 'If it's a few dollars short of twenty thousand dollars I won't go back to the bank and complain.'

The two outlaws smiled dutifully. Salmon's thoughts had wandered to consider McGee. He was probably half-way to Herford by now. Well, there was one consolation, at least one of them would have survived. He knew with a burning certainty that if anything happened to him then McGee would hunt the gang down even if it took him the rest of his life.

Glyn scuttled back in with three saddle-bags. Pope indicated that Salmon and one of the farmers should start filling them.

'And don't slip any of the money into your pockets,' said Pope, warningly.

The saddle-bags were soon filled. The last few twenty-dollar bills were transferred from the chest and stuffed inside them. The three who had been filling the saddle-bags tied them up.

'All right,' said Pope, who had been watching them carefully. 'That will do. Now you can join the others.'

The eight were lined up facing Pope and the other two outlaws.

'If you've got any last prayers,' snapped Pope, 'Now's the time to use them.'

'You're not going to kill us in cold blood,' protested one of the farmers.

'Have you got a better idea?' demanded Pope. 'You've all seen our faces. If I let you lot live then you'll go to the sheriff and give our descriptions. In a couple of days it will be telegraphed all over the territory. We won't be free for any length of time to spend the money.'

'You're not going to kill the women as well?' demanded the other farmer, with utter disbelief.

'I'm afraid so.' Pope levelled his revolver at the stage-driver. 'We'll start with you,' he said, unnecessarily.

Salmon took a step forward. Pope's gun instantly swung to cover him.

'You've forgotten one thing,' said Salmon.

'What's that?' demanded Pope, irritably.

'McGee has seen your faces. He's half-way to Herford by now. He'll be able to identify you. So there's no point in killing us.'

There was a murmur of consent from those who were about to be killed. They were willing to grasp at any straw and the one presented by Salmon seemed to have a great deal going for it.

The assembled company stared at Pope. Even his two companions gazed at him expectantly.

'You've got a point there,' Pope admitted, nodding slowly. 'After we've killed you lot, we'll have to ride into Herford and silence McGee before he says too much.'

Salmon, who a few moments ago had been congratulating himself on having extricated the assembled company from an extremely tricky situation, felt like a poker-player who had just put down four kings thinking he would scoop the jackpot, only to see his opponent lay down four aces.

'All right,' said Pope. 'All of you turn

around. I don't want to see your faces when I shoot you.'

At that moment a figure burst into the room. He, too, held a gun in his hand. It was McGee. Salmon had never been so relieved to see his friend in his life.

'If there's any shooting, I'll be the one who'll be doing it,' stated McGee. 'Just in case you don't think this gun is loaded, I'll prove it to you.'

He fired a shot at Pope's feet which hit the floor about an inch from his boot. Pope sprang back in alarm.

'Does anyone want to argue with me?' demanded McGee.

None of the robbers made a move.

8

Twenty minutes later McGee and Salmon were riding towards Herford. Their horses were carrying the saddle-bags with the $20,000 in them.

'Why did you come back?' demanded Salmon. 'I thought you were on your way to Herford.

'How could I explain to Jill that I left you with a gang of outlaws who had killed you?' demanded McGee. 'And anyhow you owe me a hundred dollars. I'll want that before you go.'

'That's what I like about you,' retorted Salmon. 'You're all heart.'

'Don't forget I was the one who got you out of that tricky situation,' replied McGee.

'I'll be eternally grateful,' said Salmon. 'And so will Jill,' he added.

They rode in silence for a while. The stage was behind them and the further they rode the distance between them and the stage increased.

'How did you manage to get hold of some bullets?' demanded Salmon. 'When you went outside the staging post your gun was empty.'

'I hung around. Then the guy who owns the staging post came into the back room to fetch the saddle-bags. He threw me a pack of bullets.'

'It was great to see the surprise on Pope's face when he realized you had got hold of some bullets.'

'It was just as good to see the pain on his face when one of the farmers tied him up. The farmer pulled the cord so tight that he almost broke Pope's bones.'

Salmon chuckled at the memory. They rode in silence for a few minutes. McGee turned around. The stage was so far behind that it was only a blur of dust on the horizon. Salmon, too, glanced around.

'Do you think we should slow down and let them catch up with us?'

'It doesn't matter if we get to Herford ahead of them,' said McGee. 'The three outlaws are trussed up like turkeys. There's no chance of them getting away.'

When they had covered another couple of miles, McGee said:

'You know what we've got in these saddle-bags, don't you?'

'Twenty thousand dollars,' stated Salmon.

'Twenty thousand dollars,' murmured McGee. 'That could make us rich men.'

'You're not thinking of stealing it, are you?' demanded Salmon, with alarm.

'Don't be stupid. We've recovered the money haven't we?'

'Yes.'

'From a robbery?'

'Yes.'

'What happens when somebody recovers some money from a robbery?'

Salmon's frank open face became creased in thought. Then he brightened.

'You get a reward,' he said, excitedly.

'Exactly. Usually you get ten per cent of the amount you saved the bank from losing.'

'Ten per cent.' There was still excitement in Salmon's voice. 'That's — let me see . . . '

'Two thousand dollars,' said McGee, impatiently.

'I was going to say that. Only you hadn't given me time to work it out. That means we'll have a thousand dollars each.'

'That's right. I think you will agree that it's not a bad sum for a day's work,' said McGee, in self-congratulatory tones.

'I will be able to buy Jill a gold brooch,' said Salmon, happily.

'And I'll be able to buy what I've always wanted,' stated McGee.

'What's that?'

'A fast stallion. A thoroughbred. One that I could train and enter for the horse races. I could even think of entering him for the Kentucky Derby.'

'Kentucky is a long way,' said

Salmon, bringing the conversation back down to earth.

'I know that. But I'll get there one day,' said McGee, positively.

Salmon glanced at him. Although they had been friends for three years, in which time they had taken part in the same circus, sometimes he felt he hardly knew McGee at all.

McGee had turned round to see whether there was any sign of the stage. Salmon copied the manoeuvre. It wasn't in sight.

'They must be a couple of miles behind us,' Salmon stated.

'We've definitely lost touch with them now,' stated McGee, as they entered a long, narrow ravine. The wheel-tracks on the dry earth showed that there was just enough room for a cart or stagecoach to drive through.

'We can't be too far from Herford,' stated Salmon. 'The feller who ran the staging post said that it was ten miles from there. And we've been riding for nearly an hour.' He glanced up at the sun as if trying to confirm his observation by its position. It stood high above the mountain rim — a dazzling yellow ball in a cloudless sky. Salmon was about to pull his hat further down on his head to shelter his eyes when he involuntarily paused.

The reason for Salmon's sudden cessation of movement could be seen in front of them. It took the form of five riders. It was obvious that they weren't on their way to a picnic since they all wore masks on their faces.

'I'm afraid I'll have to relieve you of your saddle-bags,' said the leader. 'And your guns, too.'

9

Half an hour later Salmon and McGee were in the sheriff's office in Herford. Facing them were the sheriff, Tom Milton and the deputy, Frank Gardner.

'Let's go over this again,' said Tom. 'You two say you were held up by five masked bandits.'

'That's right,' stated McGee. 'They attacked us when we rode into a narrow valley a couple of miles from here.'

'It's known as Rodney's Gulch,' supplied the deputy.

'And you say you were carrying three saddle-bags which held twenty thousand dollars which were to be delivered to a bank here,' continued the sheriff.

'That's right,' Salmon agreed. 'We took the money from three outlaws who held up the stage at the staging post.'

'You've explained how you outwitted the three outlaws. What's puzzling me is why you two didn't stay with the stage. By the way, has it come in yet?' He addressed the remark to his deputy.

'No, not yet.'

'We were quite a way in front of it,' Salmon confirmed.

'You haven't answered my question. Why didn't you wait to come in with the stage?' For the first time there was a hint of anger in the sheriff's questioning.

'We thought it would be safer if we brought it into town as quickly as we could,' said McGee.

'That was very public-spirited of you,' said the sheriff, sarcastically.

'Could it be that you two hurried into town in order to get to the bank and claim any reward that might be forthcoming for returning the money?' demanded the deputy.

The silence of the duo confirmed that the deputy might have been correct in his assumption.

'Of course, there is one other explanation,' said the sheriff, blandly.

'Another explanation?' demanded a puzzled McGee.

'If I had a suspicious mind I could say that you two rode ahead of the stage in order to steal the money.'

Salmon stared at the sheriff. He wasn't serious, was he? He was joking, wasn't he? One glance at the sheriff's face confirmed that he was indeed serious. And that in fact he was deadly serious.

McGee was the first to break the silence which had followed after the sheriff had dropped his bombshell.

'Why would we steal the money? We've already told you that we were hurrying to get to the bank so that we could claim the reward for overcoming the outlaws in the first place.'

'Well, I think your reasoning could have gone something like this. You were riding ahead of the others. You had probably assumed that you would get ten per cent of the money as a reward. That would be two thousand dollars. But as you rode along you started to think. What if you stole the whole lot. That would be twenty thousand dollars. It would set you two up for life. You could do anything you wished.'

'He could buy a ranch in Kentucky and breed horses,' said Salmon, who had been following the sheriff's reasoning with admiration.

'He could pay for his doctor's bill,' snarled McGee. 'Because he'll need one after I've finished with him.'

'Now, now, let's not quarrel,' said the sheriff, placatingly.

'I'll deal with you later,' McGee snapped at Salmon. He turned to the sheriff. 'If we invented the story of being attacked by five masked bandits, where is the money now?'

'Ah, that's the question.' The sheriff looked towards the ceiling as though seeking an answer there. When there was obviously none forthcoming from that direction he turned his attention towards Salmon, having decided that since he wasn't the brightest of the duo there was more chance of gleaning useful information from him.

'If you were to tell me where you've hidden the saddle-bags containing the money, it would save us all a great deal of time. I could even promise to put in a good word for you with the circuit judge.'

It was McGee who replied.

'You're going to charge us?' he demanded, incredulously.

'Let's say I'm not going to let you go until I get to the bottom of the whole affair.'

'But we've already explained to you what happened,' protested Salmon.

'Do you expect me to believe that the stage was held up by one gang of outlaws, then a short while later you two were held up by another gang? That is stretching credulity beyond its limits. Even Sherlock Holmes wouldn't have found that plausible.'

'Who's Sherlock Holmes?' demanded Salmon.

'He's an English fiction detective,' supplied the deputy.

'So what are you going to do?' demanded McGee.

'I'm going to keep you here until I can find out whether you two are telling the truth. There's an Indian tracker in town who will go out to the place where you say you've been ambushed. If he finds traces of five horses then, regrettably, I'll have to assume that you two have been telling the truth.'

'That seems fair enough,' concurred Salmon.

Later, when they were locked in their cell and the jailer had left them, McGee swung round to confront Salmon. He was bursting with anger.

'That seems fair enough,' he blazed. 'What the hell did you think you were doing, supporting the sheriff?'

'Well, when the Indian tracker goes out to the place where we were held up, he'll find out that we've been telling the truth,' Salmon explained reasonably as though to a small boy.

'You'd better be right.' McGee began to calm down. 'In the meantime we've got to stay in this lousy cell.'

'It's not too bad,' said Salmon. 'The mattress isn't too bad either,' he added, bouncing on it experimentally.

The sarcastic remark that sprang to McGee's lips was never uttered since there was a commotion further along the corridor. It didn't take the duo long to deduce that the three bandits who had held up the stage had arrived.

The three were locked in cells at the end of the corridor. There was a chorus of swearing as the jailer, accompanied by the deputy sheriff, locked them away. There was an empty cell between the duo and the outlaws. But any hopes that McGee harboured that somehow the three wouldn't realize that they too were in the same predicament were shattered when Pope called out:

'Hey, McGee. It's nice to know that we've got company.'

McGee kept silent. He motioned to Salmon to do the same.

'The bad news is that I know the circuit judge. His name is Warrender.

He's known as the hanging judge. He'd make the English Judge Jeffries seem like a friendly pussy-cat.'

Even in the poor light of the cell McGee could see that Salmon had paled.

'He's kidding,' McGee whispered.

'So if you've any prayers I suggest you start praying now,' was Pope's parting shot.

10

Dan Jackson surveyed the shining machine in front of him with the kind of paternal pride with which a father regards a son who has just won a game with the last kick of the match.

'Isn't he a beauty,' he purred, touching the machine reverently.

The 'beauty' would be unrecognizable to the majority of the folk of Herford as anything more than a couple of large copper cylinders connected by a copper tube. The first cylinder was arranged on a large stand below which a fire of coke was glowing. The 'beauty' stood in a large shed. The clue to its use would be seen in the dozens of stone jars which stood on the shelves. If the visitor uncorked one of the jars they would discover the distinctive smell of whiskey.

Dan hadn't addressed the remark to

himself, although lately he often found that he was guilty of talking to himself. On those particular occasions he would have had a few tastes of his whiskey — to confirm that it was just right, he would insist. This time, however, he was talking to Harold.

Harold was an Indian, who had been helping Dan for the past few months to achieve his dream of perfecting a tasty but strong bottle of whiskey.

'What do you think?' demanded Dan.

Harold took another swig at the whiskey. He smacked his lips appreciatively.

'It's great. It's the best you've made,' he added.

Dan tried his own whiskey in order to confirm the truth of Harold's statement.

'It *is* great, isn't it?' he confirmed. 'Maybe I'd better try another one just to make sure.'

He poured another glass for himself and Harold.

'This is definitely the best you've

made,' Harold confirmed.

An hour later an attractive young lady walked into the distillery. She surveyed the two inhabitants who were now lying prostrate on the floor.

'This is a nice pretty sight to come to,' she said, kicking Dan in the ribs.

His reaction was to open his eyes slowly.

'Hullo, daughter mine.' He smiled up at her. 'We've just been testing the whiskey.'

'So I see,' she said, icily.

'It's the best,' he hiccuped. 'It's the best I've made.'

'So I see.'

He pulled himself up into a sitting position with an effort.

'You said that before,' he said, accusingly.

'Aren't we observant this afternoon,' she retorted, coldly.

'Don't take that tone with me, Daisy.' His attempt at a dignified response was spoiled by the fact that he almost toppled over from his position on the floor. He hastily propped himself against the wall so that the danger of repeating the manoeuvre diminished. 'You're not too old for me to put you across my knee and give you a spanking.'

'I'm twenty-one,' she said, sharply. 'If you ever touch me, I'll walk out of here. You'll have to do your own cooking and washing and ironing and shopping. And that goes for him, too.' She kicked Harold in the ribs. Unlike her father he did not respond.

'He's out for the count,' asserted Dan.

'That's rather a pity, because the sheriff wants him.'

'What do you mean, the sheriff wants him?' demanded her puzzled father.

'He's an Indian, isn't he? He's the best tracker in Herford. The sheriff wants him for some tracking. I said I'd pass the message on. I didn't expect to find him comatose.'

'Comatose.' Dan savoured the word as if it were a new word for him.

'So what do I tell the sheriff?' demanded Daisy.

'Tell him ... ' Dan attempted to stand up. His effort would have been doomed to failure were it not for the fact that he was able to gain some support from the wall. By leaning against it heavily he was able to stand upright. 'Tell him Harold is indisposed.' He slurred that last word.

'I'll tell him the truth. I'll tell him that Harold is as drunk as a skunk.'

'I wish you wouldn't use expressions like that.' A pained expression flitted across her father's face.

'I'll just tell him he's drunk.' She paused with her hand on the doorknob. 'Do you want to know why the sheriff wants Harold?'

'You just told me. He wants some tracking done.'

'There are two fellers in jail who claim they've been held up and robbed by a gang of outlaws. The sheriff wants Harold to go out and find the tracks, to see whether the two have been telling the truth.'

'Who are these fellers? Are they local?'

'No. I saw them when they were riding in. The one's a big guy. The other's smaller — but good-looking.'

'You keep away from them — especially if they're thieves,' said Dan, warningly.

'We don't know that they are. Maybe they're telling the truth.'

'The sheriff won't have locked them up unless he thought there was something funny about their story,' stated her father.

'It's the best excitement we've had in town for weeks,' she continued. 'There are three other outlaws also locked up in the jail. They say that they held up the stage.'

'If there are five criminals in jail,' said Dan, slowly, 'that means there will be a trial. People always come in from the farms for a trial. I should be able to sell all these,' he waved an expressive hand to indicate the bottles on the shelves, 'and dozens more,' he added, enthusiastically.

'And if there's a hanging? You'll be able to sell dozens more,' was his daughter's parting shot.

11

'There are more holes in the those two guys' story than a colander,' stated the sheriff. He and his deputy were seated in his office discussing Salmon and McGee. 'In the first place how did the masked men — if they exist — know that the two of them were carrying the twenty thousand dollars in their saddle-bags?'

'Maybe they didn't know. Maybe they just held them up at random.'

'Outlaws don't hold people up by chance. This isn't England where highwaymen used to hold up travellers and say 'your money or your life'.'

'What I don't understand said the deputy, 'is why these two guys — Salmon and . . . '

'McGee,' supplied the sheriff. 'Came to Herford in the first place. They had twenty thousand dollars in the saddle-bags. If they intended stealing it, why didn't they just head off west and disappear into the sunset.'

'Maybe it wasn't like that,' said the sheriff, thoughtfully. 'Maybe they didn't decide to steal it straightaway. Maybe they had intended bringing the money in to the bank. Then, as they rode along, they began to change their minds. They began to think that twenty thousand dollars would set them up nicely for the rest of their lives.'

'So they made up the whole story.' The deputy nodded, slowly.

'Well, anyhow we'll know whether it's true when the Indian, Harold, goes to search for the tracks.'

Shortly afterwards Daisy knocked at the door and entered.

'Hullo, Daisy,' said the sheriff, pleasantly. 'Have you brought Harold back with you.'

'Not exactly.' She stood in the middle of the room, twisting her hands in front of her and looking distinctly uncomfortable.

'Where is he?' demanded the sheriff.

'He's been trying Dad's new brew of whiskey. He's drunk and he won't be sober enough to look for a trail for hours.'

'You'll have to tell your father not to try his whiskey out on him,' said the sheriff, irritably.

'He'll have sobered up by the morning,' said Daisy, hopefully.

'I suppose we'll have to wait until then,' stated the sheriff, with a sigh.

'Can I see the two prisoners. I've brought some fruit for them.' She opened a bag which she had been carrying and showed some grapes, oranges and apples.

'You're a good girl, Daisy, but you shouldn't go wasting your sympathy on two outlaws,' said the sheriff.

'I'll take you to their cell,' said the deputy. 'You can have ten minutes with them.'

McGee and Salmon were surprised

when their cell door was opened and Daisy was led into the cell by the deputy.

'You've got a visitor,' he announced. 'They say condemned men are allowed one visitor.' He chuckled at his witticism as he locked the door behind him.

'My name is Daisy,' she introduced herself. 'I've brought you some fruit.'

'That's very kind of you. I'm McGee and he's Salmon.'

'What did the deputy mean by saying we're condemned men?' demanded a worried Salmon.

'I wouldn't take too much notice of him. He was trying to be funny,' said Daisy.

'I don't think it was very funny,' stated Salmon.

McGee was peeling an orange with a penknife.

'How is it that a pretty young woman like yourself isn't married?' demanded McGee.

Daisy flushed and put her hand

behind her with its tell-tale evidence of a lack of a wedding ring.

'My father's occupation isn't exactly suitable for the likes of this town,' she said, bitterly.

'What does he do?' asked McGee.

'He makes whiskey. He's not very popular in the town. Most of the people avoid us when we meet them in the street.'

'Does he make good whiskey?' demanded Salmon, who had come out of his reverie which had been induced by the expression 'condemned men'.

'He's been trying for a couple of years, but he seems to have got it right at last. In fact his last brew was so good that the Indian who was supposed to be searching for a trail is out for the count. It will take him ages to sober up.'

'He was the one who was going to search the trail to find evidence that we've been telling the truth?' demanded McGee.

'That's right. The sheriff said that the search will have to wait until morning.'

'The evidence that there were five outlaws there could have disappeared by then,' said McGee, angrily. 'Other horses could have gone through that canyon by then and covered the tracks. And the wind could have helped to cover them as well.'

'I'm sorry,' said Daisy, inadequately.

'It's not your fault,' said McGee, magnanimously. 'It's just fate paying another dirty trick on us.'

Daisy left a few minutes later after promising to come back the following day to see whether there was anything else she could do for them.

'She likes you,' Salmon observed, after the cell door had clanged shut behind her.

'Don't talk nonsense,' said McGee, irritably.

'It's not nonsense. It was obvious from the way she kept looking at you that she likes you.'

'We've got more important things to discuss than a young girl,' retorted McGee.

'From where I was sitting I would say she's a young woman,' stated Salmon.

'Will you shut up about her?' McGee was beginning to lose his temper. 'We've got more important things to discuss.'

'Such as?' said Salmon, as he bit into an apple.

'How to escape from here.'

'Wh-at?' Salmon almost choked on his apple.

12

Daisy flung the third bucketful of water in Harold's face.

'Wake up, you lousy, good-for-nothing Indian,' she shouted.

The two previous bucketfuls of water hadn't had any effect. This one however, did seem to penetrate through to Harold's mind that there was someone who was trying to communicate with him. He still didn't open his eyes, but he shook his head and blew some of the unfamiliar wet stuff from his lips.

'If you don't wake up you'll have more of the same treatment. Only this time I'll hit you with the bucket as well,' stormed Daisy.

Whether it was the effect of the soaking or Daisy's voice screaming in his ear will never be known. However the result that Daisy had aimed at was achieved. Harold opened a bleary eye.

The sight that met the one eye was as frightening to Harold as any charge of the Seventh Cavalry to his forefathers. Daisy, beside herself with rage, was preparing to throw yet another bucketful over him. His reaction was immediate. He opened his other eye.

'Hah! So you're awake,' she yelled.

If there was one thing that scared Harold more than the sight of Daisy looking like a wild cat, it was the sound of her voice. Normally she had a low, quite pleasant voice. They would discuss any daily happenings in Herford and he couldn't remember ever being put out by her voice. But this was a rasping, strident voice pitched in a high key which seemed to shoot straight as an arrow into his befuddled brain.

'I want you cleaned up in ten minutes and ready to ride down to the sheriff's office with me.'

'I can't ride, Daisy. Not in my state,' whined Harold.

'All right, I'll take you down in the

buggy. Only get cleaned up.'

'I'll do anything you say,' Harold promised. 'Only don't shout at me,' he added.

Daisy went to harness the old mare and put her into the buggy. She was excited at the prospect of helping McGee. She was positive that he and Salmon were innocent, so all she was doing was helping the course of justice. McGee had been right when he had stated that by the next day any of the marks of the five horsemen would have been obliterated. Then there would be no proof that McGee and Salmon were telling the truth.

So you think you're doing all this to help the course of justice? said a cynical inner voice. I don't suppose it's anything to do with the fact that he's good-looking. That he's got dark wavy hair. And that he's got the deepest blue eyes you've ever seen?

He noticed that I wasn't married. That shows he's interested in me, retorted another inner voice.

Harold appeared round the corner. He looked a pitiful sight. The repeated soakings to which he had been subjected had flattened his black hair so that it appeared as though it was glued to his skull. Although he had changed his shirt and trousers, he still wore the same pair of shoes. These, too, had received some attention from Daisy's buckets of water. The result was that every step Harold took was accompanied by a slurping sound and the step was distinctly visible on the brown earth as a damp stain.

'For God's sake take your shoes off and leave them behind,' said Daisy, irritably.

A quarter of an hour later she drew up in the buggy outside the sheriff's office. Daisy entered the office with a flourish.

'I've brought Harold,' she announced. 'I've managed to sober him up.'

'I was just finishing for the day,' said a slightly surprised sheriff. Indeed it was obvious by the fact that he had donned his jacket that he was on his way out when Daisy had burst in.

'You said you wanted Harold to check the marks on the trail. If you leave it until tomorrow then it could be too late.' She couldn't keep the disappointment out of her voice.

'As I said, I've finished for the day. There's a town council meeting that I must attend. Anyhow, Frank will be in charge. You'll be in safe hands.'

I wouldn't like Frank to get his hands on me, thought Daisy. I've seen the way he's looked at me from time to time. And he's a married man with children.

Aloud she said: 'Right. I've got the buggy outside. Harold is in it.'

The sheriff left the office. Frank announced to the jail-keeper that he would be leaving the office for a couple of hours.

'Harold should just about be able to check whether McGee and Salmon's story is true before sunset,' Frank told Daisy.

They rode out to Rodney's Gulch.

Frank kept glancing behind at Daisy and Harold in the buggy.

'Can't your old mare go any faster?' he demanded, irritably.

'It's because she is old that she can't go any faster,' replied Daily. 'She'll be nineteen this year.'

'It's time she went to the knacker's yard,' said Frank, irritably.

'You're the one who should go to the knacker's yard,' replied Daisy, but in a voice low enough not to be heard by the deputy.

They eventually arrived at Rodney's Gulch.

'McGee said they had only just started coming through the canyon when they were ambushed,' Frank explained.

They went through at their usual snail's pace. Daisy kept glancing up at the sky which was already showing signs of approaching darkness. She, too, realized that if they didn't reach the spot soon where McGee had said they were attacked then it would be too dark for Harold to find any evidence.

At last they approached the far end of the canyon.

'It's somewhere around here,' Frank announced, jumping from his horse.

Harold, too, jumped down to the ground. Daisy was glad to see that he seemed quite steady on his feet. Harold began to move slowly over the ground, studying it closely.

Daisy sat impatiently in the buggy. The slowness of their progress to this spot had been nothing compared to the irritating slowness with which Harold now covered the ground. His deliberate movements were punctuated now and then by a grunt, which could mean something or nothing.

Frank was leaning against the buggy. He was smoking a foul-smelling cheroot.

'They have a dance in the church hall every Friday evening,' he said. 'I never see you there.'

'That's because I don't go,' replied Daisy, tartly.

Frank ignored her off-putting tone and continued conversationally:

'If you decide to come one Friday, save a dance for me.'

Daisy could have told him that she would love to go to the church hall dance. Not to dance with him, of course, but to have the chance of dancing with some of the other eligible bachelors in Herford. She could have told the deputy that the one thing that prevented her from going to the dance was that she didn't have a posh frock like the other young ladies. In fact she only had one frock — and that was the one she was wearing now. It was all due to their way of life, where her father had spent all their hard-earned money on a new distillery. As a result she never had any money to buy clothes like other ladies of her own age.

Her thoughts were interrupted by a shout from Harold. Unnoticed by her he had wandered off the main track and climbed a short distance up the mountainside. He had disappeared behind a large rock. He now poked his head round the side.

'This is where the five outlaws left their horses,' he announced. 'They left them here. When they came back to collect them they headed up the mountain.'

Frank and Daisy hurried to inspect the place that Harold had indicated.

'Don't come too near,' Frank warned Daisy. After the warning he proceeded cautiously towards where Harold was standing. He then crouched down to examine the tracks.

'I can see there have been some horses here,' he announced at last. 'But I can't tell how many there were.'

'There were five,' said Harold, positively. 'We Crow Indians are the best trackers in the territory. Custer always used Crow Indians for his trackers,' he concluded, with pride in his voice.

'Yes, and look what happened to him,' commented the deputy.

Daisy flashed Harold a warning

glance which said ignore the stupid idiot. Aloud she said, 'So it confirms what McGee and Salmon claimed. That they were held up by five outlaws.'

'It looks like it,' said the deputy, as he mounted his horse.

In a few minutes the procession was retracing its steps through the canyon. The only one who was excited about Harold's discovery was Daisy. Harold had already dismissed it from his mind as one more piece of evidence that the Indians were superior to the White Man. Frank, too, didn't care one way or the other whether McGee and Salmon were guilty. The sheriff would be handling the case in the morning. Any decisions to be taken, he would take them. Likewise, any plaudits to be gained out of this investigation, then the sheriff would also be the one to receive them. Even though he, Frank, had done the leg-work.

Daisy couldn't wait to arrive at the jail and tell McGee that she had helped to find the evidence which would make him a free man. She visualized his delight at hearing the news. He might take her to one of the coffee houses which were springing up in Herford. Then afterwards he would walk her home. Their cottage was a bit ramshackle compared with most of the others, but it had a porch, with honeysuckle growing over it. She and McGee would sit on the porch for a while. Then, after a few moments had passed, he would take her in his arms and kiss her. So vivid was her imagination that she could almost feel the warmth of his lips against hers.

She came out of her reverie with their arrival at the jail. Darkness had now settled in and many of the houses in Main Street had oil-lamps lit in their parlours. Daisy jumped down from the buggy almost before it stopped. Harold followed her sudden movement with surprise. She dashed into the office.

Her first inkling that something was wrong was when she saw the jail-keeper lying on the floor trussed up and with a gag over his mouth. The deputy, who was not far behind her, hastily removed the gag.

'What happened?' he demanded.

'The two outlaws in the far cell managed to escape. Somehow they managed to open the lock. I was sitting here when they burst in. The smaller one held a knife to my throat. There was nothing I could do except let them go.'

'How long ago was this?' demanded the deputy.

'Less than half an hour,' came the reply.

'Well, if they weren't guilty of taking the twenty thousand dollars, they sure were guilty of this,' said the deputy, as he cut the jail-keeper free. 'Attacking an officer of the law will get them a nice stiff jail sentence when we catch up with them.'

Daisy, who had been listening with growing horror to the jail-keeper's tale, groaned aloud.

'McGee, why didn't you wait?' she wailed.

13

McGee and Salmon were determined to put as much distance as they could between them and Herford as quickly as possible. McGee chose the route and Salmon followed him. Once they were out of the town McGee selected a mountain track. There was a full moon and so the track was comparatively easy to follow. McGee reined in his horse so that it was now proceding at a walking-pace. Salmon followed suit.

'Where are we going?' demanded Salmon.

'You'll see,' came the terse reply.

Truth to tell Salmon didn't mind where they were going. The fact that they were free was the top item on his agenda. In the end he was surprised how easy it had been for them to escape. Of course it had been McGee who had come up with the idea. They had discussed the possibility of escape after the pretty young girl had left them. The words of the deputy when he had stated that they were condemned men had stuck in his craw. What if the deputy wasn't joking, as the young lady had indicated. They were strangers in a strange town. And sometimes people got accused of crimes they hadn't committed. And even suffered the ultimate punishment of hanging as a result. He remembered vividly how he had touched his neck after the young lady had left, as if to confirm that he was really still in one piece.

So it had been with no difficulty that McGee had persuaded him that they were going to escape. The only question was how.

'You remember that escape artist who used to work with us for a while in the circus,' McGee had said.

'Yes. What was the feller's name?'

'Bandini. He had said that there wasn't a lock which couldn't be opened without a key.'

'Yes, I think I remember him saying that.'

'So here we've got a lock.' McGee pointed to the lock to the cell door. 'But we haven't got a key. So we'll put Bandini's theory into practice.'

'So what do we open it with?' demanded Salmon.

'This.' McGee produced his pen-knife.

Salmon was disappointed with McGee's suggestion.

'It might be all right for peeling an orange, but I don't think it's any good as a substitute for a key.'

'I'm not talking about the main blade. I'm talking about this.' McGee opened a blunt blade. 'This is suppose to be used for getting stones out of horses' hoofs.'

'I know. I've never seen it used yet though.'

'It can also be used as a screwdriver.' McGee applied the blunt blade to one of the screws holding the lock plate.

'It fits,' said a delighted Salmon. He

watched in eager anticipation as McGee took out one of the screws. The other three followed although the last one was stubborn and McGee had to enlist Salmon's aid to move it. Eventually the four screws had been removed, together with the back plate.

'Now the dog can see the rabbit,' said McGee, cheerfully, as he tried to turn the tumblers inside the lock.

At first there was no response. His original optimism began to change to disillusionment.

'I can't put enough pressure on it,' he announced.

'Let the expert try,' said Salmon.

He hadn't been a strong-man act for nothing. He wedged the knife inside the lock. Then he braced himself against the cell wall. He pressed hard against the knife. For a few seconds nothing happened. McGee was on the point of thinking that the whole scheme was a failure when suddenly there was a loud *click*.

'You've done it,' said a delighted

McGee. 'You've also broken my pen-knife,' he added, as Salmon handed the mangled instrument back to him.

'Some people are never grateful,' observed Salmon.

Overpowering the surprised jail-keeper was easy. Their horses were in the compound at the back of the jail and collecting them and putting saddles on them only took a matter of minutes. So here they were riding along a mountain track. Now and again McGee kept glancing down at the valley below.

'We're not lost are we?' demanded Salmon, when they had been riding for about half an hour.

'Of course we're not lost,' snapped McGee.

Salmon's faith in McGee was still holding up. After all, his companion had got them out of the cell. They were riding in the cool night air. They were free men. True, it was rather chilly up here in the mountains, but the main thing was that they could see the track clearly. That meant that there was no danger of the horses stumbling.

During those moments when he gave some thought to the direction in which they were heading Salmon concluded that they were heading south. He had deduced this because he had glimpsed the North Star behind them. True, the North Star was the only one in the sky that Salmon recognized, but at times like this when they were heading into darkness where there was not a single light in sight, it gave him a modicum of comfort to know in which direction they were heading.

At some time during the next half-hour the knowledge that they were heading south prompted another thought. Why were they heading south? The basic idea of getting away from Herford was flawless. It was to be fully applauded. On a scale of one to ten that basic assumption would receive top marks every time. To get as far away from Herford as possible was an escapist's aim. But why were they going south when he would have thought they should have been going north?

He decided to question McGee.

'We're heading back towards Stoneville,' he stated.

'I know,' said McGee.

'Shouldn't we be going the other way?'

'No,' said McGee.

Salmon reflected that he hadn't learnt much from the conversation. Except that McGee was in fact leading them back towards Stoneville. The place where they had started out from yesterday. Was it only yesterday? It seemed like ages. McGee suddenly veered to the right to follow another track. Salmon obediently followed him.

They were now descending from the mountain. Salmon could see the valley floor below. It must be the same valley that they had come along when they left the stage behind and ended up in Herford.

When they reached the valley floor McGee urged his horse into a steady gallop. Salmon followed suit. This time they were able to ride side by side. The moon still obligingly provided enough light for them to maintain their fairly rapid progress.

Salmon had some questions to ask McGee. In fact the questions increased with every mile. But when he looked across at McGee's set face he decided to leave the questions until later. McGee was staring ahead like a ship's captain searching the horizon for any signs of the enemy.

They rode in silence. Salmon had lost track of time. What time had it been when they had escaped from the jail. Ten o'clock? Yes, that was probably about it, since it was already dark. How long had they been riding? At least two hours by his reckoning. Of course the first hour or so had been fairly slow since they had been on the mountain track. But since then they had been galloping at a steady pace.

Salmon was suddenly struck by an idea. He knew now where they were heading for. It was obvious that they were going back to Stoneville. The problem he had imagined to exist wasn't really a problem at all. He had assumed that they were still wanted by the law, since the sheriff in Herford had wrongly accused them of stealing the twenty thousand dollars. But they hadn't appeared in a court of law before a judge and so they really hadn't been charged with any crime. Up to now he had assumed that the sheriff in Herford would want them back to face the charges. But he had overlooked one thing — the sheriff didn't know where to find them. True, they had given their names as Salmon and McGee, but they hadn't said where they lived. He could see it all now. They were heading south. They would jump on the train at the first railway station they came to. Then they would make their way to New York. They would disappear into the crowds. The sheriff of Herford would never find them in a hundred years. He would be reunited with his beloved Jill and their son, Henry. This trip to

Herford would be as something which hadn't happened.

He was so engrossed in his pleasant thoughts of being reunited with Jill that he hadn't taken much notice during the past ten minutes or so where they had been heading. He suddenly realized that they were approaching the staging post. It was lit by a solitary lamp in one of the bedroom windows. Well, they certainly wouldn't want to stop here. The last thing they would want to do would be to meet anyone who could identify them. They needed to remain as anonymous as possible — at least until they could board the train heading south.

They approached the staging post with the horses at a walking-pace. McGee was scanning the horses in the compound. Surely he wasn't thinking of stealing one of the horses, was he? They were in enough trouble with the law as it was. The last thing they wanted was to be labelled as horse-thieves. He knew that they hung horse-thieves. They were considered, next to murderers, as the worst criminals.

McGee had jumped down from his horse. Why had he done that? Surely the main object was to go past the house and get back to Stoneville as quickly as possibly. McGee motioned to Salmon to get from his horse. He reluctantly obeyed.

McGee walked up to the front door. To Salmon's horror he began to bang on it. Was McGee going out of his mind?

There was no immediate response from inside the house. McGee banged on the door again. This time it did produce a response. Salmon could see that the lamp which had been in the bedroom window had suddenly disappeared. He guessed that the person holding it was coming down the stairs.

McGee then did something which Salmon found even more puzzling. He drew his revolver. A few moments later a voice from inside said:

'Who's there?'

Salmon recognized it as Glyn's, the staging-post keeper.

'It's me, McGee,' came the reply. 'I've got a message from your friends.'

There was a pause. 'All right, I'll open the door. But I warn you that I'll have got you covered.'

While the bolts were being drawn McGee motioned to Salmon to draw his gun. Salmon obeyed.

When the door was eventually opened the staging-post keeper was revealed holding a lamp in one hand and a revolver in the other.

'I think you'd better put that revolver away,' said McGee. 'We're both sharp-shooters.'

The keeper held up his lamp to see the duo more clearly. The action confirmed that there were two revolvers against his one. He tossed his gun away.

Salmon could contain his curiosity no longer.

'Will you tell me what's going on?' he cried.

'Our friend here will explain every-thing,' said McGee, pushing past Glyn and going into the house.

14

The following morning a strange sight met the sheriff when he turned up at his office. Already seated there were his deputy and McGee and Salmon. The fourth person, though, he failed to recognize.

'What's this, a committee meeting?' he demanded, icily.

'These three were here when I arrived,' explained the deputy. 'Two of them you know. This guy,' he pointed to the proprietor of the staging-post, 'is called Glyn Canning.'

'Right. Will someone explain what this is all about?' the sheriff demanded.

The deputy coughed, showing that he was going to start.

'Last night, these two escaped from prison. They tied Charlie up and rode off into the night. I never thought I'd see them again.'

'So you went away and came back?' demanded a puzzled sheriff.

McGee took up the story.

'I'm sorry about the jail-keeper. But we didn't hurt him. We only tied him up. I wanted to get to the staging-post as quickly as I could, but it was too late. The birds had flown.'

'What birds?' demanded the sheriff.

'The five who held us up. You see, the puzzling thing was, how did they know that we were carrying the twenty thousand dollars to bring to the bank. There could only have been one explanation.'

'That you made the whole thing up,' suggested the sheriff.

'No, we found evidence — or rather Harold found evidence that there were indeed five riders hiding behind a large rock in Rodney's Gulch,' stated the deputy.

'All right, so your story is true,' conceded the sheriff. 'Then how did the five outlaws know that you two were carrying the money?'

'He told him,' said McGee, pointing to Glyn.

'But I thought that the stage wasn't far behind you. How did he manage to get ahead of you and tell the outlaws that you two were coming?' demanded the sheriff.

'He knew that the five outlaws were waiting in the canyon to rob the stage. Of course the money wasn't on the stage. So he had to ride ahead of us to warn his friends. He set out while the three who are in the cells were being tied up. Nobody noticed that he had gone. He took the mountain track which we rode along last night. He reached the outlaws about ten minutes before we did. The rest you know,' said McGee.

'Is this true?' demanded the sheriff, eyeing Glyn who was almost trembling with fear.

'Yes, it's all true. I warned them that these two were carrying the money. But I never took part in the robbery. Honestly.'

'So you know all about the five robbers?' said the sheriff, thoughtfully.

'Yes. I can give you their names. And their descriptions,' said Glyn eagerly. 'That will count in my favour won't it, if it comes to court.'

'I can't promise you anything. But I'd definitely mention it to the judge,' said the sheriff.

Half an hour later McGee and Salmon were seated in one of the coffee houses. Salmon was on his fourth slice of apple tart while McGee was sipping his coffee reflectively.

'I still don't know how you worked it out,' said Salmon, wiping a few crumbs from his chin.

'It had to be the guy who owns the staging post. He was the only one who could have ridden in front of us and told the outlaws that we were bringing the money,' explained McGee.

'I'd never have thought of it in a million years,' confessed Salmon.

'The question is, what are we going to do next?' said McGee, thoughtfully.

'The sheriff said he'd like us to stick around for a few days in case they caught up with any members of the gang. Then we'd be able to give evidence against them,' stated Salmon.

'The problem is we're short of money,' said McGee. 'We've got enough for a couple of nights in a saloon. After that we'll either have to move on or find some work.'

'If we'd only had that two thousand dollars reward for bringing in the money to the bank,' sighed Salmon.

'It's all water under the bridge now,' stated McGee.

At that moment his attention was drawn to somebody tapping on the window of the coffee house. It was Daisy.

'Your girlfriend wants to see you,' Salmon announced.

'She did make the deputy sheriff ride out to confirm our story about the outlaws,' stated McGee, as he went outside to greet her.

'You're free,' said a delighted Daisy.

Before McGee could reply she kissed him on the lips. It was a lingering kiss which brought a few disapproving stares from some of the women who were passing on the sidewalk.

'My father would like you to join him in celebrating your freedom,' she said. 'He says he's just brewed the best whiskey in the territory.'

'How can we refuse such an offer?' said McGee.

Daisy contentedly tucked her arm into his as they headed towards her house.

15

In the town of Crichton which was about twenty miles from Stoneville, Jill and Letitia, Salmon's and McGee's wives, were studying a newspaper. They were reading it at a railway station while waiting for their train to New York. From the expression on their faces the item of news they were studying wasn't exactly the most cheerful. In fact it was bordering on the tragic.

'We can't go there now,' Jill wailed.

'The paper is dated the beginning of the week,' stated Letitia. 'That means the epidemic is still active.'

'We can't risk our babies catching such a disease,' said Jill.

'Never mind about our babies, what about us?' demanded Letitia. 'We could catch it if we went to New York.'

'What about our parents, they could have caught it.' Jill started to sob.

'They've probably gone to Connecticut to escape it,' said Letitia, reassuringly. She reread the item of news on the front page. Under the heading, EPIDEMIC HITS NEW YORK, it described how a smallpox epidemic had hit the city. It stated that at present seventy-six people had died of the disease. And there were hundreds of other suspected cases. It added that thousands of people were fleeing from New York to try to avoid catching the disease.

'If we can't go to New York, what do we do now?' asked Jill, drying her eyes.

'We go back to Stoneville,' said Letitia, positively. 'We'll have to take the children back there. Won't their fathers be surprised!'

In fact the fathers were enjoying some of the best whiskey they had ever tasted.

'This is great,' enthused McGee.

Dan Jackson regarded McGee in much the same way as a great painter might regard an art connoisseur who has just praised his latest picture.

'It's the best I've made,' said Dan, proudly.

'It's the new distillery,' said Daisy. Her voice, too, echoed her father's pride.

'It's great,' remarked Salmon.

'So what are you two thinking of doing next?' demanded Dan, as he refilled their glasses.

'We haven't decided,' said McGee.

'I hear you're a pair of sharpshooters,' said Dan.

'Yes, we used to work in a circus in New York,' admitted Salmon.

'Why don't you two put on your act in the town square? Daisy could collect your money.'

'Hey, that's a great idea,' enthused Daisy.

'We could always try a couple of performances to see how they go,' said McGee.

'We're supposed to be on our way to Chicago,' Salmon reminded him.

'We can always go to Chicago later,' said McGee.

'Why are you going to Chicago?' demanded Daisy, trying unsuccessfully to hide her disappointment at the news.

'Salmon wants to buy a present for his wife,' said McGee, quickly.

'So you're married, then?' enquired Dan.

'Salmon is,' McGee cut in quickly. Salmon's face took on a shocked expression at the implication that McGee himself wasn't married. To create a distraction McGee added, 'Do they get many people in the town square?'

'They will tomorrow, since it's market day,' said Dan. 'What I was thinking of doing was selling my whiskey after you two had performed your act.'

'It sounds reasonable to us,' stated McGee.

Salmon, who was still smarting at McGee's insinuation that he wasn't married, said nothing.

'Then that's settled,' said Dan. 'I think we should have another drink to celebrate.'

Daisy came around with the bottle and poured their drinks. As she poured McGee's drink she held his hand in hers while she slowly poured the whiskey. The gesture wasn't lost on Salmon.

'Have you two decided where you're going to stay tonight?' asked Dan.

'We'll have to find a saloon,' said Salmon.

'I can't recommend the place where we spent last night,' said McGee.

Dan smiled. Daisy laughed as though it was the best joke she had heard for ages.

'If you don't want to go to a saloon, there's a spare bedroom in the house,' said Dan. 'It's empty, but you can put your saddles there and use your blankets.'

'That'll suit us,' said Salmon. 'We were used to sleeping rough when we were working as cowboys in Stoneville.'

'You can sleep in the bedroom,' said McGee. 'I'll sleep out here in the open. I'll get more sleep this way than listening to you snoring all night.'

At first Salmon accepted the suggestion. Then he glanced at Daisy and intercepted a knowing glance between McGee and her. It was the sort of glance which said: since you'll be out here in the open I'll have a chance to visit you tonight.

Salmon stood up. 'Before we turn in, we'll see to our horses,' he announced.

When the two were out of earshot of Dan and Daisy, Salmon turned fiercely on McGee.

'What do you think you're playing at?' he snapped.

'What do you mean?'

'Don't play the innocent with me. I know why you're staying out here in the open. So that Daisy can come and keep you company. Have you forgotten that you're a married man?'

'It's only a harmless bit of fun,' said McGee. 'A few kisses and cuddles, that's all.'

'And what if Letitia finds out about

your 'fun'? She's got a temper like a wild cat.'

'She'll never find out,' said McGee airily. 'She's half-way to New York by now.'

'I wouldn't like to be in your shoes if she does find out,' was Salmon's parting shot.

16

In Herford five men were strolling around the town. To all intents and purposes they were just casual visitors. They were obviously not cowboys since they were all wearing suits. If anyone had taken a good look at them the person could have deduced that the five belonged to the constantly shifting population of people who were making a quick dollar by fair means or foul. The five could have been professional gamblers. They had that indefinable air of people who lived by their wits. In fact anyone who had come up with that conclusion would not have been far wrong, since two of the five, Shaw and Potter, were in fact professional gamblers. Of late they had forsaken their gambling to take up the more lucrative pastime of robbery. The five had been responsible for holding up McGee and

Salmon and riding off with $20,000.

'This money's burning a hole in my pocket,' said one of the gang. He was the smallest of the five, named Downs.

'Four thousand dollars,' said Todd. In any test of the intelligence of the five robbers he would have come out at the bottom of the list. He was slow of thought and speech. However he was a big man and so it was an unwritten rule that nobody ever mentioned his lack of intelligence. If they did they would be in danger of having their arm broken.

Shaw and Potter, since they had something in common — their gambling — had teamed up from the moment they had joined the Staple gang six months before. They were walking together along the sidewalk.

'Four thousand dollars,' stated Shaw. He was older than Potter. In fact the reason he had joined the gang was that he had realized that he was getting too old for gambling. To be a successful gambler you had to have extremely sharp reactions. You had to arrive at split-second decisions. You had to see things that the others in the card-school would have missed. You also had to know how to cheat. The last time he had joined in a card-school he had in fact been cheating. He had only been saved from an unpleasant sojourn in the nearby jail by the intervention of Potter, who had happened to be in the card-school at the time. While the other players had sworn that Shaw had been cheating, Potter defended him, saying that there was no way Shaw could have been cheating. The other players had wavered, then eventually decided to take no action against Shaw. The result was the card-school had broken up. Shaw had bought Potter a drink. They had become friends, despite the difference in their ages. And shortly afterwards they had joined Staple's gang.

Staple himself was rather a puzzle to the other members of the gang. Most of the time he presented a tall, taciturn front who only spoke when he had something important to communicate. He was a born leader and none of the gang ever questioned any of his decisions. On one occasion when there had been a disagreement over some minor issue or other he had instantly flared up. In fact his behaviour had seemed in such complete contrast to his normal quiet demeanour that the members of the gang had been taken completely by surprise. Staple had ranted and raved until at last the members of the gang had managed to pacify him. After that the members of the gang made doubly sure that they did not contradict him — not even on the smallest matter.

They were passing a saloon.

'Let's go in and have a drink,' suggested Downs.

'All right,' conceded Staple. 'But no more than a couple of drinks. I don't want you lot flashing your money around. If you do it could mean that all of us could end up in jail. And I don't propose spending the rest of my life in one of those stinking places.'

The others were surprised by the vehemence of his outburst. However they filed into the saloon without further comment.

Downs walked up to the bar and ordered five beers.

While the barman was pulling the drinks he asked pleasantly:

'You fellers staying in town?'

'No, we're just passing through,' said Staple, sharply.

The barman put the drinks on the bar in front of them.

'I was only asking because I've got a couple of rooms spare,' stated the barman.

'As I said, we're just passing through,' stated Staple, in a conciliatory tone. He put a twenty-dollar bill on the counter.

'We don't get too many of these,' announced the barman. He picked it up. For a moment it appeared as though he was about to put it in the drawer. Then abruptly he changed his mind. He examined the bill again. This time more closely.

He turned to Staple.

'I'm afraid I'll have to ask you for payment in smaller notes or in coins.'

'What's the matter? Don't you take large notes?' sneered Staple.

'I don't mind taking large notes,' replied the barman. 'But not ones that are forged.'

'What do you mean, forged?' Staple examined the note that the barman was holding up.

'Look at it,' said the barman. 'It's not even a good forgery. The ink has already started to run.'

Staple examined the bill. The others joined in the examination, the expression of disbelief on the faces being almost comical to witness.

Staple tossed a few coins on to the bar to pay for their drinks. He carried his own drink to a quiet corner and the others followed suit.

'You know what this means,' he stated.

'That one of the bills was forged,'

suggested Todd.

'All the bills have been forged, you fool,' Staple hissed.

Todd flushed. His other reaction was to clench and unclench his fist.

'I don't understand how we've come to be carrying forged notes,' stated a puzzled Potter.

'It's obvious,' snapped Staple. 'The people at the bank in Stoneville were expecting to be robbed. They sent a consignment of forged notes hoping that if we took them we would try to get rid of them in one of the large shops where it would be obvious we had lots of the forged notes. Then they would call the sheriff. Luckily we only changed one of them here. And I don't think the barman is suspicious. It's all the fault of those two guys, McGee and Salmon,' he ended, viciously.

'How do they come into it?' demanded Shaw.

'They set the whole thing up. They were working for the bank in Stoneville. They brought the notes and handed them to us on a plate. That should have told me that there was something about them in the first place.'

'You mean the genuine money stayed in the bank in Stoneville,' suggested Downs.

'Of course not,' snapped Staple. 'Those two guys brought the real money with them. It was probably hidden in three saddle-bags exactly like the three the guys handed over so willingly to us.'

'Then where is it now?' demanded Potter.

'That's what we aim to find out. The two must be still here in Herford. We will split up and look for them. With luck we might catch them before they have taken the money to the bank.'

'What do we do if we see them?' said Todd.

'You've all got guns,' stated Staple. 'Bring them back here. We'll meet here at noon.'

17

McGee, Salmon, Dan and Daisy set out for the market square. Dan was driving the buggy which was well stocked with his bottles of whiskey. Salmon was walking alongside the horse, having deliberately distanced himself from McGee and Daisy, who were walking hand in hand behind.

'This should be a good day for us,' said Dan, enthusiastically. 'When you two guys finish your sharpshooting act, I'll step in and start selling my whiskey.'

'What about the women?' demanded Salmon. 'We've seen whiskey sellers before who've been run out of town by the women.'

'Oh, I've been selling whiskey here for months,' replied Dan, airily. 'Nobody's tried to run us out of town yet. By the way, how's your head after trying my samples last night?'

'It's not too bad,' admitted Salmon. 'In fact it's a lot better than I would have thought. I can't speak for him of course.' He jerked a dismissive thumb in the direction of McGee.

'He seems to be enjoying himself, anyhow,' observed Dan.

McGee and Daisy were in fact happily chatting together.

'I expect you've had lots of girl-friends,' suggested Daisy.

'One or two,' admitted McGee. It was not a subject he was anxious to pursue.

'I had a boyfriend until a few weeks ago,' admitted Daisy.

McGee contributed a nondescript grunt hoping that it would discourage Daisy from continuing with the subject.

'His name was Luke. He was a big guy — almost as big as Salmon. But he was too . . . ' she searched for the word, 'possessive. That's why I finished with him.'

'Sometimes it's often a good idea to have a change,' McGee agreed, blandly.

'The other thing about Luke was that he was so immature. Even though he was a couple of years older than me. I prefer my men to be more experienced.' She clung even more tightly to McGee's arm.

Salmon, who had overheard the last remark, threw a comment over his shoulder.

'Yes, he's had plenty of experience.'

Daisy accepted the remark at its face value.

'I don't even mind my man to be older than me,' she stated.

'Hey! I'm not that old,' protested McGee.

They had arrived at the town square. Unlike many towns in the West the original settlers had foreseen that the town might one day expand. With that in mind they had built a sizable square which had four roads leading off it. These were actually near enough to the points of the compass and the old folk would point out to their grandchildren that you could never get lost in Herford since one of the roads leading from the square was named West Street. So if you went in the opposite direction you would be going east. Similarly if you turned left off West Street you would be going north. If you went in the opposite direction you would be going south. And it was from that direction that Downs came and spotted McGee and Salmon.

Dan had drawn up the buggy in a corner of the square. Daisy had helped him to set up a makeshift shelf on which they were loading their bottles of whiskey. Downs correctly assumed that the four would be in the square for some time. He calculated this would give him enough time to find suitable help from other members of the gang. He turned and hurried back in the direction from which he had come.

Herford was quite a big town and it took Downs a quarter of an hour before he came across another member of the gang. To his relief it turned out to be Staple. He quickly explained the situation and they hurried back towards the square.

McGee and Salmon had finished their sharpshooting routine by the time they arrived. Daisy was collecting the money.

'There must be over twenty dollars here,' she said, as she handed the money to McGee. 'You've got enough to take me out tonight,' she added, suggestively.

'I'll think about it,' said McGee as he pocketed the money.

The duo's sharpshooting had attracted a fairly large crowd. Now it was Dan's turn to sell his whiskey.

'You all know me,' he began. 'My name is Dan. I'm Dan, Dan the Whiskey Man.' This brought some appreciative laughter from the audience. They were already in a good mood from watching the duo's sharpshooting and so were prepared to listen to Dan's speech. He praised his latest whiskey, stressing its beneficial medicinal effects more than its obvious alcohol qualities. In the end many of the men stepped forward eagerly to buy the bottles at five dollars each.

Daisy was busy handing them out and taking payments for them. Two men who had been watching with interest were Downs and Staple. In fact they had now been joined by Shaw who had happened to arrive on the scene.

In a short while Dan had sold all his bottles.

'I'll have to go back to the house and bottle some more,' he announced happily.

'I'll come with you,' said Salmon.

'Daisy and I are going for a stroll around town,' said McGee. 'If she's a good girl I might even buy her a present.'

'I'm always a good girl. That's my trouble,' said Daisy, as she slipped her arm into McGee's.

The two set off for Main Street, which boasted the largest stores. They were closely followed by Staple, Downs and Shaw.

'The biggest store in town is called Rodders,' said Daisy, excitedly. 'They've got some lovely things there.'

'Then that's where we're going,' stated McGee. 'You can buy whatever you wish. Within reason,' he added.

They entered the store with the three outlaws following close behind. It soon became obvious to McGee that Daisy was going to take some time in choosing a present, in fact a considerable amount of time. He soon became bored with waiting while she searched through scarves and jewellery. When she went into the ladies' underwear section his patience finally became exhausted.

'I'm going into the coffee shop to wait for you,' he announced. He handed her five dollars. 'This is to buy yourself a present.'

'Thanks, McGee,' she said, her eyes shining with happiness.

No sooner had McGee disappeared in the direction of the coffee shop than three men gathered around Daisy. At first she took no notice of them, assuming that they were merely customers like herself. However when one of them produced a revolver from under his jacket her eyes widened. Her expression changed to a startled one and then to fear when he hissed:

'You're coming with us, young lady. If you scream I will shoot you. I've killed several people in my lifetime and one more won't make much difference.'

Daisy immediately knew from the hardness in Staple's voice and the coldness of his eyes that he meant what he said.

18

Letitia and Jill finally arrived back in Stoneville. They were weary, hungry and dusty and, on top of that, both their offspring had spent much of the last few hours doing what young babies are good at — crying.

'I can't wait to get into a hot tub,' said Jill. 'When I get into it, I'll stay there for hours.'

'I can't wait to see McGee again,' said Letitia. 'I can just imagine his face when he sees that we've come back so soon.'

In fact it was Letitia's face which registered stunned shock when they reached their landlady's house and Mrs Crabtree informed them that their menfolk had gone.

'Gone?' said a disbelieving Letitia.

'Where to?' asked Jill.

'They didn't say,' said Mrs Crabtree.

'Although I heard Mr McGee say that they might be away for as long as three months.'

'Three months,' howled Jill. 'What were they going to do for three months?'

'They didn't say,' reiterated Mrs Crabtree.

Letitia paced up and down the room. 'Three months. That sounds suspiciously like the time they thought we'd be away in New York staying with our parents.'

'How could they do this to us?' Jill began to cry.

'Hush, you'll wake the babies,' said Letitia, automatically.

'They'll be half-way to wherever they're going by now.' Jill began to dry her eyes, sniffing as she did so.

'I bet I know where they are heading for,' Letitia announced. She stopped pacing.

'Where?' demanded Jill.

'Chicago.'

'Why do you think they've gone

there?' demanded Jill.

'It's obvious, isn't it?' stated Letitia. 'They said they could be away three months. That means they will be travelling a good distance. They'll be going to a large town where McGee can carry on with his favourite pastime.'

'What's that?' demanded Mrs Crabtree, who had been an interested audience to the conversation.

'Gambling,' snapped Letitia. 'The only reason he hasn't been able to gamble here is that there aren't any big-time gamblers to make up a card-school.'

'He did start a card-school with the cowboys who worked in the same ranch as himself and Salmon,' Jill pointed out.

'Yes, and the first time they played he won all their weekly wages. They wouldn't play with him after that,' said Letitia.

'I'm not surprised,' said Mrs Crabtree.

A few hours later they had an unexpected visitor. It was the deputy sheriff.

'I heard that you two ladies were back in town,' he said, addressing Letitia and Jill.

'I suppose you've heard, too, that our husbands have disappeared,' said Letitia, tartly.

'Yes, they caught the stage two days ago,' said the deputy.

'Do you know where they went?' demanded an excited Jill.

'They went to Herford. That's as far as the stage goes. Of course they might have intended to go on from there.'

'How could they do this to us?' Jill was almost in tears.

'What do you mean 'intended'?' Letitia had caught the implication in the deputy's words.

'Well, that's the point,' said the deputy. For the first time since entering Mrs Crabtree's house he began to look uncomfortable. He was fidgeting with his hat.

'What do you know about them?' insisted Letitia.

'Well, ma'am, we've had a telegram

from the sheriff of Herford saying that McGee and Salmon are in jail.'

'In jail?' repeated a shocked Jill.

'What are they in jail for?' demanded Letitia.

'The telegram doesn't say. It just said they were in jail and that the sheriff would appreciate any information about them that we could send.'

'Can you send a telegram back asking why they're in jail?' demanded Jill.

'I'm afraid it's too late now,' said the deputy. 'The telegraph office is closed for the day. Of course, we can send one first thing in the morning.'

He left shortly afterwards, having refused Mrs Crabtree's offer of a cup of coffee. The landlady herself went into the kitchen to prepare the dinner. Left on their own the two wives discussed what they were going to do about their husbands.

'There's nothing we can do,' said Jill. 'We'll have to wait until tomorrow so that the telegraph clerk can send a telegram.'

'You know how long that's going to take,' retorted Letitia. 'We'll be lucky if we get a reply by the following day.'

'Well there's nothing else we can do,' said a resigned Jill.

'Oh yes there is,' said Letitia. 'We can catch the stage first thing in the morning. We'll be in Herford by the early afternoon. We can turn up at the jail and find out exactly what's been going on.'

Jill was about to argue with her friend. But one look at the steely determination on Letitia's face dissuaded her. She consoled herself with the thought that if they went to Herford she would be able to see her beloved husband.

'I'd better start getting things ready,' said Jill.

* * *

Daisy, too, was panicking about her future or possibly a lack of it if the outlaws carried out their threat. They

133

were camped in a glade in a wood which was half-way up the mountain-side.

'I tell you McGee doesn't have any money,' she protested for the umpteenth time. 'He's only got the money that they took this morning in the market place. He gave me five dollars to buy a present. Do you think that's all he would have given me if he had twenty thousand dollars as you say.'

'You'd be the last person he'd want to tell about his money,' sneered Staple. 'He knows you'd only spend it.'

Daisy tried once again.

'Why don't you let me go free? I could find out if McGee really has got the money. If he has I could let you know.'

'I've thought of a better idea,' said Staple. 'I've told McGee that if he doesn't come up with the money in two hours then you'll be killed.'

Daisy did what many other young women would have done in the circumstances. She fainted.

19

McGee was desperately searching for Daisy. What could have happened to her? He went into each department in the store asking the same question.

'Have you seen a young girl. About twenty. She was wearing a yellow dress with small red flowers on it. She is quite pretty with long dark hair.'

He met the same blank stare accompanied by head-shaking every time. He went back into the coffee house and asked the same question. Again he was met with the same head-shaking.

In desperation he even tried a couple of the nearby stores, thinking that possibly she might have changed her mind and gone into one of them. Still he met with no success.

In the end McGee decided to go back to Daisy's house. As he walked slowly along the street he wondered gloomily what he would be able to tell Dan. How do you tell a father that his daughter has suddenly disappeared? That in fact the man who was supposed to be looking after her was in a coffee shop while he should have been by her side.

As he walked he kept glancing around as if half-expecting to see her suddenly materializing. In the end he had to conclude that she had just disappeared. His footsteps slowed even more as he approached the house.

When he reached the door he took a deep breath and knocked. Dan opened it. To McGee's surprise, Dan was holding up a piece of paper.

'Is this true?' demanded Dan.

'Is what true?' asked a puzzled McGee.

'That Daisy has been kidnapped and she is being held by some outlaws.'

McGee took the paper from Dan and read it.

It said: *We've got your girlfriend,*

McGee. We want the twenty thousand dollars you've swindled us out of.

'What twenty thousand dollars?' demanded McGee.

'That's exactly what I said,' supplied Salmon who had materialized by Dan's side.

'Then what's this guy talking about,' said Dan, with desperation in his voice.

'Who brought this note?' demanded McGee.

'He was a small guy;' said Salmon. 'He said his name was Downs.'

'There's only one thing to do,' said McGee. 'We'll have to go to the sheriff. He'll have to get a posse together to find Daisy.'

'There's no chance of that,' said Dan, glumly. 'Downs said they'd start cutting off Daisy's fingers if we went to the sheriff.'

McGee digested the bad news. Eventually he said:

'What else did this guy say?'

'He said that he'd be back in two hours. If you didn't come up with the twenty thousand dollars he'd kill Daisy.' He choked on the last words.

'What are we going to do?' demanded Salmon.

'I'll have to have time to think,' said McGee.

'Don't take too long,' said Dan, wildly. 'If you don't come up with something they're going to kill my Daisy.'

20

Salmon and Dan were looking expectantly at McGee. When Dan had explained that Daisy would be killed if they didn't come up with the $20,000 McGee had gone into a trance. He had stared in front of him as if the other two didn't exist. Dan, who had been surprised at McGee's reaction, glanced for an explanation towards Salmon. But the other merely shrugged his shoulders.

McGee had been in his uncommunicative state for several minutes. When it didn't seem as though he was going to break the silence, Salmon took the bull by the horns.

'What are we going to do?' he demanded.

'There's only one thing we can do,' replied McGee.

Dan, relieved that McGee had once

again become a normal human being, said:

'Then there *is* something we can do?'

'Of course there is,' said McGee, impatiently.

'If there is a way out then McGee will find it,' stated Salmon, with the positive air of a preacher for the Seventh Day Adventists.

'Then what do we do?' demanded Dan.

'We rob a bank,' stated McGee, flatly.

'What?' Salmon almost jumped out of his skin.

'It's the only way out,' said McGee, with passion. 'We rob a bank. We give the money to these guys. Then they'll release Daisy.'

Salmon, who was slowly recovering from a state of shock at hearing McGee's suggestion said:

'He's out of his mind.'

'I thought you said he would come up with a suggestion,' snapped Dan.

'He usually does,' said Salmon, who felt that it was his duty to defend his friend even though he had gone completely mad.

'Then when we hand the money over we follow the guy with the money and get Daisy released.'

'If there's anybody going to see about getting Daisy released, it'll be me,' said Dan, belligerently.

'You'll be needed for something else,' stated McGee.

'What's that?' demanded Dan, suspiciously.

'You'll be getting in touch with the sheriff to explain what's happened. The gang won't be watching the sheriff's office once they've got the money. The sheriff will be able to get his posse and catch them.'

Silence descended while the two digested McGee's plan.

'It might work,' Dan said at last.

'It doesn't stand a chance,' protested Salmon.

'You're sharpshooters. You should be able to rob a bank,' stated Dan, persuasively.

'We've always kept within the law,' protested Salmon. 'And anyhow they hang bank-robbers.'

'If they get caught,' said McGee, airily.

'Are you going to help McGee to rob the bank or not?' demanded Dan. 'If not I'll have to help him. And I'm not very good with a gun.'

'Of course he'll help,' said McGee, positively. 'He's never let me down yet.'

'Maybe we'll get lucky and only be sentenced to life imprisonment,' said Salmon, gloomily. 'Then my son can come and visit his old father in jail.'

McGee ignored him. 'There's one thing we've got to decide,' he said.

'What's that?' demanded Dan.

'You know the town. Which bank is the easiest to rob?'

'It's got to be the Western National,' stated Dan, without hesitation. 'It's off Main Street — it's in West Street. It hasn't got a guard — just an old man who used to be in the army back in the Civil War.'

'It sounds ideal,' stated McGee. 'There's only one other thing.'

'What's that?' asked Dan.

'You'd better put our names down for the lunatic asylum,' interrupted Salmon. 'Because nobody will believe that we robbed a bank in order to give the money to some other bank-robbers.'

'Ignore him,' said McGee. 'He'll be all right once we're on our way.'

'You said there was something else,' Dan reminded McGee.

'That's right. We'll want masks. Just as a precaution.'

'That won't be any problem,' Dan assured him. 'Is there anything else you want.'

'Only our heads examined,' supplied Salmon.

21

Letitia and Jill had arrived at the staging house between Stoneville and Herford. The stage had made its usual halt and the passengers had disembarked. Both Letitia's and Jill's offspring had been perfectly behaved while in the stage. In fact, possibly lulled by the movement of the stage, they had both slept nearly all the way.

They were greeted by the buxom proprietress.

'We don't often see children on the stage,' she stated.

'We'll feed them while the others are having their meal,' explained Jill. 'Is there a separate room we can use?'

'There's a small room at the side.' She ushered Jill and Letitia into the room. 'I'll bring you some coffee,' she added.

'Well, we're half-way to Herford,' said Letitia. 'Although goodness knows what we'll find when we get there.'

'If Salmon and McGee are in jail,' stated Jill, 'I'm sure it's a misunderstanding. Salmon would never do anything which meant him breaking the law.'

At that moment Glyn, the proprietor entered the room. He was surprised to see Letitia and Jill who were feeding their babies.

'The lady who runs the place said we could use this room,' Letitia explained.

'It's all right,' he said. 'We don't often get babies in here. Robbers yes, but not babies.'

'What do you mean, robbers?' demanded an instantly alert Letitia.

'Bank-robbers,' he elaborated.

'When was this?' pursued Letitia.

'The last time the stage came through. Two days ago.'

'That would have been when Salmon and McGee were on the stage,' exclaimed Jill.

'You know those two guys?' demanded Glyn.

'They're our husbands,' stated Letitia.

'Well, fancy that,' he said in surprised tones.

At that moment his wife brought in the coffee.

'Do you know that these two ladies are married to the two men who helped to foil the hold-up here a couple of days ago?' he exclaimed.

'They managed to foil a hold-up? But we heard they were in jail,' said a puzzled Letitia.

'Three men held up the stage while it was here,' explained Glyn. 'McGee managed to get away. Then, while I was getting some rope to tie up the passengers, McGee managed to slip back. I gave him some bullets and he was able to turn the tables on the robbers. In the end they were the ones who were tied up with the rope I had brought.'

'He was a hero!' exclaimed a delighted Letitia.

'But why did they end up in jail?' demanded Jill.

'The incredible part is there was a second robbery,' said Glyn.

'A second robbery?' echoed a bemused Letitia.

'McGee and Salmon had taken the twenty thousand dollars that the robbers had stolen from the stagecoach. They were riding into Herford with it. Obviously intending to deposit it in the bank. When they were a couple of miles this side of Herford they were held up by another gang of outlaws.'

'A nice friendly neighbourhood you've got here, with all these bank-robbers milling about,' said Letitia.

'What happened next?' demanded Jill.

'McGee and Salmon handed over the twenty thousand dollars. The robbers rode off with the money. McGee and Salmon went into Herford. They explained to the sheriff that they didn't have the money they were supposed to be bringing in for the bank.'

'I don't suppose that went down very

well,' stated Letitia.

'It didn't. The sheriff put them in jail.'

'But they were obviously telling the truth,' protested Jill. 'So they're still in jail?' demanded Letitia.

'As far as I know,' said Glyn. He deliberately failed to mention the part he had played in the second robbery. He didn't mention how McGee and Salmon had ridden out to the staging post and confronted him. That he had been forced at gun-point to confess his contribution to the second hold-up. That he had then been forced to ride with the duo into Herford. That he had fully explained to the sheriff his part in the robbery. That he was only free at the moment because the sheriff would be depending on his evidence to hang the bank-robbers once they were caught.

At that moment the driver of the stage entered.

'If you two ladies are ready, we're all set to start,' he announced.

'We can't get to Herford quickly enough,' stated Jill.

'Although goodness knows what we'll find when we get there,' added Letitia.

22

In the sheriff's office, Tom Milton was discussing with his deputy, Frank, the latest development in the 'case of the bank-robbers' as he called it.

'So that's what it's all about,' he concluded.

'So the saloonkeeper said,' stated Frank.

The saloonkeeper in question had left their office a couple of minutes before. He had given his evidence, then informed them that he was in a hurry to get back to his saloon because he didn't know what mischief the young lad whom he had left in charge could do while he was away. The sheriff had told him to get back to his saloon since he knew where he could find him when the necessity arose.

'Forged twenty-dollar notes,' announced the sheriff.

'You would have thought the bank should have told us that they were sending forged notes in their last delivery.' There was annoyance in Frank's voice.

'If they'd sent us a telegram, somebody in the telegraph office might have been hand-in-glove with the gang and they might have warned the gang that there was no point in holding up the stage since the notes were forged,' said Tom.

'I suppose so,' admitted his deputy. 'Although we're not any nearer to catching any of the five robbers.'

'We've got three of the other gang in jail,' Tom reminded him.

'Yes, that's thanks to McGee and Salmon. If they hadn't turned the tables on the first gang then things would have worked out differently.'

'They should have had some sort of reward for that,' said the sheriff, thoughtfully. 'Maybe I'll have a word with the bank manager and explain that they are two public-spirited men who deserve a reward for overcoming the first bank-robbers. By the way, where are they now? Are they still in town?'

'Oh, yes. They did their sharpshooting act in the square a few hours back. Dan — the man who makes the whiskey — was with them. When they had finished their act he managed to sell quite a few bottles of his latest brew.'

'I suppose you managed to get one?'

'Yes, I was lucky.'

'Next time they're in the square, see that you get one for me.'

*　*　*

His whiskey, however, was the furthest thing from Dan's mind as, together with McGee and Salmon he prepared to rob the bank. They had tied up their horses in a lane by the side of the bank.

'I chose this because it's a nice quiet place,' Dan informed them.

'Put your masks on,' said McGee.

They obeyed and when McGee drew

his revolver the others followed suit.

'I've never done this sort of thing before,' whispered Dan.

'Do you think we have?' countered Salmon.

'Ready?' demanded McGee. The two signified that they were.

They marched into the bank brandishing their guns.

'This is a hold-up,' said McGee. 'If you give us the money in the safe nobody will get hurt.'

There were four people in the bank, two behind the counter and two in front of it. One of the men in the front of the bank said:

'Don't shoot anybody. I've got an elderly mother to support and I don't want to get hurt.'

'Nobody will get hurt,' said McGee. 'As long as the two behind the counter open the safe and put their money into these.'

He tossed two saddle-bags over the counter.

The younger of the two bank clerks

grabbed the saddle-bags.

'Shall I do as they say, sir?' he demanded.

'Of course you'll do as they say, Rawlings,' said the other, who was obviously the bank manager. 'We don't want anyone to get hurt do we?'

The fourth person in the bank voiced his feelings.

'We don't want any shooting,' he concurred.

Everything seemed to be going smoothly. McGee's only concern was that somebody might decide to come into the bank and interrupt the proceedings.

Salmon and Dan watched in silence as the bank clerk and the manager filled the saddle-bags. Dan pondered McGee's instruction not to say a word once they were inside the bank. Of course in his case it made sense; it meant that nobody would be able to recognize his voice if ever they were found out. Although the way things were going at the moment it looked as though they were going to get away with it after all. One saddle-bag was already full and the two men behind the counter had started filling the second.

Salmon, too, was wondering about McGee's instruction about speaking. Of course it made sense not to say anything, since in the first place it was difficult to speak wearing a mask. What was puzzling him was the remark which McGee had insisted he should utter. It didn't make any sense to him. Still McGee always seemed to know what he was doing.

Sweat was standing out on the brows of the manager and the clerk as they filled the bags.

'You'll never get away with this you know,' said the manager.

McGee did not reply.

The saddle-bags were almost full.

'When we leave,' said McGee, 'Nobody moves for five minutes. One of us will still be outside seeing that you obey this instruction. Do you understand?'

'We'll do anything you say, as long as

there's no shooting,' said the old man.

'I agree with him,' said the other.

The bank manager and the clerk finished filling the saddle-bags. Salmon picked them up.

Then Salmon uttered the words which McGee had told him to utter.

'Come on, Downs,' he cried. 'Let's go.'

23

Daisy had never been so depressed in her life. It all hinged on a statement from Shaw, one of the oldest members of the Staple gang. While they were waiting for McGee and Salmon to bring the money, he had been the only member of the gang who had been concerned about Daisy's predicament.

'I've got a daughter of my own. She's about your age,' he had confessed to her, when he had sat on the grass near her.

'I bet she isn't being held captive by some robbers,' she snapped.

'I can understand why you're feeling annoyed,' he said, taking out a packet of tobacco and beginning to roll out a cigarette.

'Can you? Do you know what it feels like to be held prisoner, not knowing what's going to happen next?' She was shouting now.

Staple called across. 'Shut that girl up, or I'll shut her up myself.'

'He means it,' whispered Shaw. 'If you don't keep quiet he'll crack you on the head and tie you up until the money arrives.'

'I keep telling you that McGee hasn't got the money,' she protested, vehemently. 'He gave me five dollars to buy a present. Does that seem like someone who has got twenty thousand dollars?'

'He'd better turn up with something, or you'll be in trouble. Did you say his name is McGee?' he added.

'Yes, he's a short guy. He's handsome,' she added, dreamily.

'I know him,' replied Shaw. 'I met him once. There can't be too many McGees around. Is he a gambler?'

'I think he likes to play cards. I've heard him talk to his friend Salmon about some card-games they've been in.'

'That's them,' said Shaw, excitedly.

'McGee and Salmon. Salmon's a big guy, isn't he? As big as Todd.'

Daisy glanced across to where the four outlaws were seated, playing cards.

'Yes, I suppose so.'

'I knew I was right. I met them when I was gambling in New York. McGee and Salmon are well-known gamblers.'

'McGee might have been a gambler in New York but I'm sure I can help him to reform,' she said, with all the determination of youth.

'Charlie the Hook,' said Shaw, reminiscently. 'It's coming back to me now.'

'Who's Charlie the Hook?'

'He's a big-time gambler. And I mean a real big-time gambler.'

'Why do they call him Charlie the Hook?'

'Because he has a hook instead of his left hand. But he can still deal aces off the bottom of the deck with his right hand.'

'So McGee lost a small sum of money to Charlie the Hook? That's not the end of the world.'

Shaw began to laugh. He laughed so much that he doubled up with the effort. The card-players glanced across at him.

'If you don't stop making so much noise, I'll silence you as well,' snapped Staple.

The threat was enough to silence Shaw.

'So what's funny?' demanded Daisy, irritably.

'McGee didn't owe Charlie the Hook a small sum of money. He owed him five thousand dollars.'

'What?' Daisy was so shocked that she stood up.

'Sit down.' Shaw grabbed her and forced her to sit down again. 'You must sit down or they'll think you're trying to escape.'

'Are you sure?' demanded Daisy, grasping at a straw that perhaps the information that she had received was somehow false.

'Positive. The news was all over every

gambling-school in New York. That's why McGee and Salmon came out West. If Charlie the Hook had caught up with them their bodies would have been found floating down the Hudson River.'

'Maybe he'll give up gambling.' She was still clinging to the straw, hoping against hope that McGee was still the kind of perfect man in her life that she had dreamed of.

'Gamblers never give up,' said Shaw, positively. 'Look at me. I've sworn on dozens of occasions that I would never gamble any more. But if you put a deck of cards in front of me and bet me that you'll cut a higher card than me, I'll put all my money on the cut without thinking twice about it.'

'McGee is different,' she said, stubbornly.

'Yes, he's different all right. He's married and I'm not.'

'What?' She was about to shoot up again, but he grasped her hand. After a brief struggle he forced her to sit down.

161

'It's not true,' she said, wildly. 'He said he loves me.'

'Of course he'd say that. Men often say that when they want to get their own way.'

'Are you sure he's married?' She was close to tears.

'I'm positive. They used to work for a circus in New York. His wife's name was Lotty — no — I've got it. Letitia.'

Daisy began to sob.

'If you don't shut that girl up,' yelled Staple, 'I'll shut her up for good.'

'If you do, you'll be doing me a favour,' sobbed Daisy.

24

The stage had arrived in Herford. Letitia and Jill, since they were carrying their babies, were the last to leave.

'Where do we go to now?' demanded Jill.

'To see the sheriff, of course,' replied Letitia. 'We've got to find out where our men are.'

They found the sheriff's office without any difficulty. The sheriff welcomed them with a smile.

'What can I do for you ladies?' he asked.

'We're looking for our husbands,' replied Letitia.

Frank, the deputy, was regarding the babies suspiciously. Unlike his superior he didn't have any children, and so wasn't too familiar with young babies.

'Who are they?' he demanded.

'Salmon and McGee,' replied Jill.

Surprise registered on the faces of the sheriff and his deputy.

'We were talking about them earlier,' said the sheriff.

'Where are they now?' demanded Letitia, with more than a note of urgency in her voice.

'We're not quite sure,' said Frank. 'The last time we heard of them they were helping to sell whiskey in the town square.'

'I'll give him selling whiskey.' Letitia flared up angrily. 'We came all the way here thinking they were in jail. And what do we find? That they're selling whiskey. And sampling some of the stock in the process, no doubt.'

'It *is* good whiskey,' Frank averred.

The sheriff's glance of disapproval wasn't observed by the ladies since at that moment the door burst open. A man who was perspiring freely stood there. A quarter of an hour before he had been inside his bank filling the saddle-bags for the three robbers.

'What's the matter, Percy?' demanded

the sheriff. 'You look as though your bank has been robbed.'

'It has,' replied the bank manager. The deputy fetched another chair and he sank gratefully into it.

'You'd better tell me about it, Percy,' prompted the sheriff.

'We were held up about half an hour ago by three men. They said they wanted all the money that was in the safe. Me and my clerk filled their saddle-bags as they instructed, then they rode off.'

'Could you identify them?' asked the deputy.

'No, they all wore masks. One of them, though, was a big guy, and another was a small one.'

Letitia and Jill paled. Their reactions weren't lost on the sheriff.

'You think two of them might have been Salmon and McGee?' he demanded.

'Oh, no,' replied Letitia, hastily. 'I'm sure our husbands wouldn't get involved in robbing a bank.'

'And anyway, one of the men said that the name of the small guy was Downs, not McGee,' supplied the bank manager.

At that moment Harold the Indian burst into the office.

'I've got an urgent message,' he cried.

'Don't say there's something wrong with Dan's next brew of whiskey,' said Frank.

The sheriff scowled at his deputy's attempt at humour.

'Well let's hear it,' he said.

'Dan's daughter, Daisy has been kidnapped by some outlaws. Dan and McGee and Salmon have ridden out to rescue her. If you follow them you'll catch the outlaws.'

'Why should they kidnap Daisy?' asked a puzzled sheriff.

'I don't know. I was just told to give you the message,' said Harold.

'You say that Dan and McGee and Salmon have ridden out to rescue her,' said the deputy. 'How are we going to follow them? The outlaws could be holed up anywhere.'

'Dan loosened a nail on one of his horse's shoes. It will make a distinctive mark. I should be able to track it.'

'It sounds like a good idea,' said the sheriff.

'McGee thought of it,' replied Harold.

'He would,' said Letitia.

'How long have the gang been holding Daisy?' demanded the deputy.

Harold shrugged. 'An hour? Two hours?'

'Could these outlaws have any connection with the gang who robbed my bank?' enquired the bank manager.

'I doubt it,' said the sheriff. He stood up. 'Well we've got work to do.' He addressed Letitia and Jill. 'If you will excuse us, ladies.'

'See that Salmon and McGee don't come to any harm,' said Jill.

'I'm sure McGee can look after himself,' retorted Letitia, as they left the sheriff's office.

25

McGee, Salmon and Dan were indeed on their way to the outlaws' hiding-place. Downs had turned up at Dan's house within the two hours as he had promised.

'Have you got the money?' he demanded.

'Yes, we've got the money.' McGee had taken over the role of spokesman.

'Right. If you'll hand it over, I'll take it back with me. Daisy will be released as soon as I get back to the camp.'

'Not so fast,' said McGee. 'How do we know that you're going to keep your end of the bargain and release Daisy.'

'What would we want your girlfriend for?' demanded a puzzled Downs.

'Let's say that we don't trust you,' replied McGee. 'So we're coming with you.'

'All three of you?' asked Downs, with

mounting concern.

'I'm her father,' stated Dan.

'And where McGee goes I go,' announced Salmon.

Downs was clearly unhappy with the arrangement. He made one last effort to appeal to their better judgement.

'Why won't you trust me to send Daisy back home?'

'You're a bank robber,' supplied McGee. 'Your type are the last people on earth we'd want to trust.'

Salmon burst into a bout of coughing. Downs took advantage of the interlude to glance inside the saddle-bags.

'Is all the money here?' he demanded.

'You can count it when we get to your camp,' stated Dan, who felt that he was being neglected, since McGee had obviously taken charge of the proceedings.

Downs saw no way out of the present position.

'All right, you three can come with me. But you'll leave your guns behind.'

He watched while the three took their guns out of their holsters and tossed them on to the table.

'How will we defend ourselves if we're attacked by outlaws?' asked McGee.

'Very funny,' sneered Downs.

'I hope you know what you're doing,' Dan whispered to McGee, as they went outside to get their horses.

'He always comes up smelling of roses,' stated Salmon.

'That will be enough talking from you three,' snapped Downs. 'We'll all of us ride quietly to our camp.'

They started off at a steady pace. Instead of riding through the town, Downs took a side road. They were obviously heading for the mountain which lay ahead. Suddenly McGee pulled his horse up.

'What's the matter?' demanded Downs, irritably.

'There's something wrong with my horse.'

McGee dismounted. He examined

each shoe in turn. When he came to the fourth hoof he exclaimed:

'She's lost one of the nails in her shoe. You three had better go on. I'll go back to the house.'

'Oh, no you don't,' replied Downs, sharply. 'You're coming with us. If I leave you behind there's nothing stopping you going to the sheriff. You know in which direction our camp lies. The sheriff could get a posse together and hunt us down before we could get very far from the town.'

'What do you suggest?' demanded McGee, innocently.

'You're coming with us. Your horse will slow us all down, but we'll just have to put up with it.'

So the four set off once again, this time at a definitely slower pace. They eventually reached the lower slopes of the mountain.

'How far do we have to go?' demanded McGee. 'My horse is having difficulty with its faulty shoe.'

'It's not far. The camp is up in those

trees.' Downs pointed to a copse about 1,000 feet up the mountainside. While his attention was distracted McGee dropped his tobacco tin among the long grass.

They proceeded at their slow pace. Their lack of speed irritated Downs.

'Can't you go any faster?' he demanded.

'This is as fast as I can go,' replied McGee. 'Anyhow, you said that it's not far.'

'I'm glad that it isn't. If we were going any distance I'd shoot your horse,' said Downs.

As they rode McGee kept his gaze fixed on the copse ahead.

'I can't see any signs of your friends yet. Are you sure they're in there?'

'Of course they are. They're camped in the trees at the other side.'

They reached the copse at last and started to ride through it. After a while they came to a clearing. There were a group of men sitting around on the grass.

'We're here,' said Downs, unnecessarily.

Staple stood up.

'What did you bring those three for?' he demanded.

'They insisted on coming,' replied Downs. 'They said they wanted to see that the girl was safe and sound.'

'She's safe enough. In fact we'll be glad to get rid of her. All she's been doing is howling. I've had to tie her up and gag her to shut her up.'

'You haven't harmed her, have you?' Dan involuntarily moved towards his daughter.

'Stay where you are.' Staple levelled his gun at him. 'Of course I haven't harmed her.'

Although Daisy was trussed up she managed to nod her head to show that she was all right.

'Is this the money?' Staple was examining the two saddle-bags.

'That's right. Twenty thousand dollars.'

Staple was still flicking through the money.

'There doesn't seem as much as that here.'

173

'If you don't believe me, why don't you count it?' suggested McGee.

Staple was clearly unhappy about the quantity of notes in the saddle-bags.

'Come on, boss,' said Potter. 'If it's a few dollars short it won't make any difference. There's plenty there for a five-way split.'

'What's the matter,' prompted McGee. 'Do you think we might have kept some of the money for ourselves?'

Staple flushed. 'I'm not having these three guys making a fool of me by keeping some of the money,' he snapped. 'I'm going to count it.'

'We'll want a table or something to count the money on,' said Downs. 'Let's just take the money and get out of here.'

'I'm in charge here,' stormed Staple. 'If I say we're going to count the money, then we're going to count the money. There must be something flat around here that we can count the money on,' he added, looking round for any ideas.

The blank expressions on the outlaws' faces told him that they didn't have any ideas.

'You'll just have to give up the whole idea,' McGee goaded him.

'Don't you tell me what to do,' screamed Staple. 'We'll count the money the hard way. Potter, hold out your hand.'

Potter obeyed.

Staple picked out a bundle of notes from one of the saddle-bags. Then he started counting them one at a time into Potter's hand. When he reached a hundred dollars Potter would transfer the money into an empty saddle-bag and one of the others made a notch in a stick to signify each hundred.

McGee strolled across to where Daisy was sitting. Staple watched him warily but didn't stop putting the notes into Potter's hand. McGee untied the gag from round Daisy's mouth. Her reaction took him by surprise. She spat in his eye.

For a few moments McGee was

nonplussed. Then realization dawned.

'You found out that I'm married.'

'Of course I did. You skunk. You worm. You snake in the grass.' She racked her brains thinking of other invectives.

'I can't be a snake in the grass and a worm. The snake would have eaten the worm.'

'I never want to speak to you again.' She turned her head away from him.

'Listen Daisy, I'm sorry I deceived you. When we get out of this you can hit me or kick me, or do anything you like to me. But you want to see these outlaws punished, don't you?'

Daisy nodded.

'Right, then this is what you will do.' McGee whispered urgently in her ear.

It was taking some time to count the money. The other outlaws were getting restless. A couple of them went to the edge of the clearing to tend to their horses. Shaw came over to talk to McGee.

'I don't know whether you remember me, but I met you in New York,' he said,

176

conversationally.

McGee studied his face then shook his head.

'No, I'm sorry, I can't remember meeting you.'

'It was in a saloon on Broadway. You were playing in a heavy gambling-school. It was too expensive for me. I was just watching.'

'Was the place called *Marnie's*?'

'Yes, that's right. If I remember rightly you won five thousand dollars that night.'

'And lost it all the following night,' said Salmon, who had come to join in the conversation.

Staple was coming to the end of counting the money. The two outlaws who had been tending the horses came back to find out the result.

Staple was counting the last bundle of notes into Potter's hand. Every pair of eyes was glued on the last handful of notes. The exception was McGee, who seemed to be having trouble with his boot.

The last note was placed into Potter's hand.

'Sixty-four,' intoned Staple. He glanced at Downs who had been cutting the number of hundred dollars into a stick.

Downs added up the number of notches. At every tenth notch he had cut a larger one to denote that he had reached a 1,000. The whole gathering held their collective breath while he counted.

Eventually he announced the result. 'Eighteen thousand, five hundred and seventy-three dollars.'

'Eighteen thousand, five hundred and seventy-three dollars. Are you sure?' demanded Staple.

'I'm positive,' replied Downs. 'I used to work in a bank. I don't make mistakes counting money.'

Staple swung round to face McGee.

'Where's the rest of the money?' he snarled. 'You owe us one thousand five hundred dollars.'

'One thousand, four hundred and twenty-seven dollars,' said McGee, mildly.

'All right, smart guy, I'm asking you where it is,' Staple shouted.

'I haven't got it. You can search me.' McGee showed the palms of his hands in the universal gesture of innocence.

'If you don't come up with a better answer than that, you'll be on your way to meet your maker.' Staple's cocked gun emphasized the point.

'No, don't kill him.' It was an involuntary cry from Daisy.

'You've got nearly all the money,' said McGee, persuasively. 'Why don't you leave it at that?'

'Nobody cheats me and gets away with it.' This time Staple was shouting at the top of his voice.

The outlaws looked at each other apprehensively. They had seen Staple in this mad mood before and it had always boded ill for the person who had been responsible for starting it.

'I'm going to count up to three.' Staple's voice was calmer. 'If you don't tell me where the missing money is then you know what will happen. One — '

Daisy sobbed quietly.

'I don't know where it is. If I did do you think I wouldn't tell you?' Suddenly McGee's face twisted as though in pain.

'Two — '

McGee's reaction was startling. He fell on the ground. Not only did he fall, but he began to writhe in agony.

'I've got the cramp,' he cried.

The assembled company watched him as he twisted and spun on the ground.

'Finish him off and let's go,' said Todd.

'I can't finish him of while he's wriggling around like this,' snapped Staple.

If anything McGee's contortions had increased. He spun, twisted and turned with such rapidity that Staple, having tried to take aim at his head had in the end given up the idea. He held his gun loosely in his hand while waiting for McGee to come up off the ground.

When McGee did so it was in one

rapid movement. Staple's reaction was slow. His revolver was on its way to its firing position when the knife which McGee had produced from his boot went unerringly into his heart.

'You've killed him,' announced Todd, unnecessarily.

The outlaws had all drawn their guns and were facing McGee, Salmon, Dan and Daisy.

'You don't think you are going to get away with it,' said Todd, who had suddenly become the gang's spokesman.

'I don't see why not,' replied McGee. 'If you listen I think you will find that the cavalry have arrived.'

As if on cue there was the sound of horses coming through the trees. The outlaws didn't know how many men they would have to face. Added to which they were now leaderless. The result was their guns froze in their hands.

The sheriff, the deputy and half a dozen men carrying rifles burst into the glade. They took in the assembled company.

'All right. Drop your guns,' commanded the sheriff.

'Are we glad to see you,' said Dan.

McGee went over to Daisy and began to untie her.

'You're not spitting at me this time?' he asked.

'That was a brave thing you did,' she said. 'It was foolish though.'

'I thought the odds were in my favour.'

The comment brought a begrudging smile from Daisy.

'What's all this money?' demanded the sheriff.

'It's eighteen thousand, five hundred and seventy three dollars,' supplied Salmon.

'That's the exact sum which was stolen from my bank.'

The bank manager had materialized, having kept a safe distance behind the posse.

'So you outlaws stole the money,'

said the sheriff, reflectively.

'No, we didn't,' protested Todd. 'We've been here all the time.'

'Why don't you tell the sheriff the truth, Downs,' said McGee. 'You went into Herford and robbed the bank this afternoon.'

'No, we didn't,' said Downs, wildly. 'As Todd said, we've been here all the afternoon.'

'Downs,' said the bank manager, excitedly. 'That was the name of one of the robbers. He turned to Todd. 'And you were the right size to be the other guy in the bank.'

'I tell you we were all here,' cried Shaw. 'Daisy will confirm it.'

Daisy, who had been rubbing her hands to restore the circulation glanced around slowly. The assembled company were all hanging on her statement. She savoured her moment of importance to the full. She glanced around like a queen about to deliver a proclamation. When her words eventually came they caused instant consternation.

'Shaw was here with me all the afternoon,' she replied. 'All the others went into town for a couple of hours. When they returned they brought this money with them.'

There were vociferous denials of Daisy's interpretation of events.

'She's lying,' cried Downs.

Potter went to draw the knife in his belt with the obvious intention of using it.

'Go on. Draw it,' said McGee. Harold, when he had arrived on the scene, had given McGee his revolvers. 'You saw how fast I was with a knife,' added McGee. 'I'm even faster with a gun.'

'He is,' Salmon confirmed.

* * *

The outlaws' surprise at Daisy's interpretation of the events of the afternoon paled into insignificance when compared to McGee's and Salmon's reaction on arriving in the sheriff s office and seeing

184

their wives and offspring.

Letitia and Jill smiled at their husbands' reactions.

'For once he's at a loss for words,' said Letitia, as they met their husbands with the kind of kisses which hinted that there were more to come later.

Daisy, who was also in the party, turned away with embarrassment.

When he drew away, McGee introduced Daisy.

'I'm pleased to meet any acquaintance of McGee's,' she stated. 'Particularly his wife.'

'We've got a lot of work to do,' announced the sheriff. 'Why don't all of you go to a coffee house. If you come back in, say, half an hour my deputy will take down your statements.'

'How long in prison do you think the four will get?' asked Dan, as they made their way out.

'It's hard to say,' replied the sheriff. 'Stealing twenty thousand dollars from the bank is a serious crime. I'd guess they'd get at least ten years each.'

'At the trial I'd like to put in a good word for Shaw,' said Daisy. 'He's an old man. He was kind to me when the robbers had tied me up.'

'By the way, why exactly did they tie you up?' demanded the deputy.

'Didn't we tell you?' replied Daisy, serenely. 'The gang wanted to know the secret of Dad's latest brew of whiskey. They all say it's going to be a world-beater.'

When they were on their way to the coffee house McGee slipped in by Daisy's side.

'Daisy, I must congratulate you. You are a magnificent liar.'

'Coming from you, that's praise indeed,' she replied.

THE END

We do hope that you have enjoyed reading this large print book.

Did you know that all of our titles are available for purchase?

We publish a wide range of high quality large print books including:
Romances, Mysteries, Classics
General Fiction
Non Fiction and Westerns

Special interest titles available in large print are:
The Little Oxford Dictionary
Music Book, Song Book
Hymn Book, Service Book

Also available from us courtesy of Oxford University Press:
Young Readers' Dictionary
(large print edition)
Young Readers' Thesaurus
(large print edition)

For further information or a free brochure, please contact us at:
Ulverscroft Large Print Books Ltd.,
The Green, Bradgate Road, Anstey,
Leicester, LE7 7FU, England.
Tel: (00 44) 0116 236 4325
Fax: (00 44) 0116 234 0205

LOBO AND HAWK

Jake Douglas

One was a Yankee. One was a Rebel. They were the only two survivors of the bombardment of a New Mexico town at the end of the Civil War. After trying unsuccessfully to kill each other, they decided to become partners and go after some Confederate gold that was up for grabs. The trouble was that they weren't the only ones who knew about the hoard. Soon there would be trouble enough to bring back old hostilites, and only blazing guns would settle the matter. But who would live?

HIGH STAKES SHOWDOWN

Mike Redmond

The placid work routine at the Ferguson Ranch is abruptly shattered one afternoon when young cattleman Matt Farrell discovers a dead body on the range and simultaneously finds himself at odds with the foreman, McCoy, over the favours of old Ferguson's feisty daughter, Hetty. Now a breathless sequence of events finds Farrell braving a lynch mob, defending himself in a brutal bare-knuckled fight and facing death in a final shootout in a spooky Arizona ghost town . . .

THE GUN MASTER

Luther Chance

They lived in the shadow of a fear that grew by the hour, dreading the moment when their world would be destroyed by a torrent of looting and murder. And when that day finally dawned, the folk of Peppersville knew they would be standing alone against the notorious Drayton Gang. There was not a gun in town that could match the likes of the hard-bitten, hate-spitting raiders. But now it looked as if change was on the way with the arrival of the new schoolteacher, the mysterious McCreedy . . .

KINSELLA'S REVENGE

Mark Falcon

Newton, Kansas, was a cow town in 1871, when bounty hunter twin brothers Fin and Ray Kinsella became involved in what was to be called 'the Newton General Massacre'. It was to lead Ray on the road to revenge. Along the way, Ray and the three-man posse met up with Kitty Brown, sole survivor of a family murdered by one of the men they were tracking. She joined the posse on a ride that would change all their lives. And, when the shooting stopped, revenge from beyond the grave would come to haunt them all.

HELL'S BACK DOOR

Vic J. Hanson

Stark City was a hell-hole of a prison, set in the desert and run by the vicious Captain Hector Stark. And amongst the motley bunch of criminals was the legendary Clay Dachin, an educated man but reputedly a cold-eyed killer. No prisoners had ever escaped and survived, but Clay was determined to break the pattern and gathered a formidable bunch of men around him. Could they escape and beat the relentless desert? Or would Clay, like an earlier prisoner, end up with his head stuffed, as the Captain's trophy?